The Extinction of Rhinos in Mexico

THE EXTINCTION OF RHINOS IN MEXICO

9 Tales of Life and Death

[signed] Stephen Blackburn

STEPHEN BLACKBURN

Copyright © 2001 by Stephen Blackburn.

Library of Congress Number: 00-193354
ISBN #:   Softcover   0-7388-4477-2

All rights reserved. No part of this book may be reproduced or transmitted in any form or by any means, electronic or mechanical, including photocopying, recording, or by any information storage and retrieval system, without permission in writing from the copyright owner.

This collection of stories is a work of fiction. Any references to historical events; to real people, living or dead; or to real locales, are intended only to give the fiction a setting in historical reality. Other names, characters, places, and incidents are either the products of the author's imagination or are used fictitiously, and their resemblance, if any, to real-life counterparts is entirely coincidental.

This book was printed in the United States of America.

To order additional copies of this book, contact:
Xlibris Corporation
1-888-7-XLIBRIS
www.Xlibris.com
Orders@Xlibris.com

CONTENTS

webs center 13

The Extinction of Rhinos in Mexico 18

Ordeal of the Arrow 38

Meat Caves 50

Orion's Belt 85

The Smell of a Christian 102

Carrion Birds 148

Pagar Por Sustos 160

Guardian 190

Cover Art: Untitled colored woodcut by C. A. Manzaroli.
Cover art photographed by Melinda Briana Epler. TIFF file created by Joshua Warner.
Author Photograph: T. David

This book is for my nieces Chelsea, Corey *and* Kandace, *and for my nephew* Dylan.

PREFACE

James Michener's first book of fiction, a collection of short stories titled *Tales of the South Pacific*, wasn't published until he was forty years old, and he then proceeded to enjoy a successful career spanning nearly fifty years, two facts which spur aspiring writers everywhere. By the time *The Extinction of Rhinos In Mexico* is published, I will be forty-five years old. This is my first book of fiction, and it is being published by me through Xlibris, one of several companies riding the new wave of computerized publishing technology. Print on Demand (POD) companies are a democratizing development I believe Mr. Michener would have relished.

James Michener had done a fair amount of living by the time *Tales of the South Pacific* hit the bookshelves, so he well understood how precious a commodity time is for a writer, the more so for an unestablished one trying to squeeze in an hour of writing around a day job. I have earned my living variously as a university teaching assistant, industrial video producer, cook and dishwasher, warehouse forklift driver, researcher for a screenwriter, immigration petition writer for a law firm, stagehand and spotlight operator, convention decorator, movie extra, contracts data entry consultant for a movie company, and scaffold builder at major construction sites. Among other things. I once had a temp job where I sat in the back of a big rig for hours with a load that had shifted, and by hand put beer cans back into the plastic six-pack rings. That should give you some idea just how invaluable and idyllic were the two years provided me by the James Michener Fellowship program at the University of Texas in Austin.

I'm fortunate enough to have met Mr. Michener a couple of years before he died. There were ten of us, giddy (at least I was) from being freshly selected for the privilege of actually being paid to write full time (and work toward a Master of

Fine Arts). We arrived for our audience with the Great Man, and were ushered by his personal assistant to a small parlor just inside the front door of Michener's Austin home. There we sat waiting, all dressed up, occasionally speaking in hushed voices and fidgeting in our good clothes like kids at church. By and by, here came Mr. Michener, nearly ninety, moving slowly but under his own steam, wearing Bermuda shorts, sport shoes, t-shirt, bathrobe and a NASA baseball cap. He greeted us all informally and took a seat at one end of the room. I don't remember what particular words of wisdom he may well have imparted to our group, but I do recall that he spoke with each of us in turn. He asked us what we were writing, listened with interest, and then exhorted us to stay the course. His health was already failing, but his spirit remained vigorous, his mind keenly engaging the world. He was still writing.

The stories in this book are largely the product of my two years as a Michener Fellow. "Orion's Belt" was the short story that got me into the program; "The Extinction of Rhinos In Mexico" was my thesis short story. "Meat Caves," "Carrion Birds," and "Guardian" were all workshopped in Austin. "Guardian" I read to audiences at Austin's Hyde Park Theater on two occasions; that experience helped me hone the story and converted me to the practice of reading stories aloud as part of my creative procedure. I have tinkered with most of these stories over the past couple of years, fine-tuning them. The lengthy process has put a new slant on my appreciation for time as an important element in writing. Sometimes a story pours out of you, as was the case with "Rhinos" and "Pagar Por Sustos," but a lot of times a tale has to simmer in first, second or tenth draft for a long while before you can ultimately distill its best resolution. All of these stories have benefitted from my returning to them over time, fixing a phrase here, a word there, shifting scenes to different locations, or even having some wholly new and fortuitous realization that puts the

THE EXTINCTION OF RHINOS IN MEXICO

luster on a story.

By endowing the Texas Center for Writers (posthumously renamed the Michener Center for Writers), James Michener and his wife Mari provided a magnificent legacy of generosity that will be bolstering aspiring writers for generations to come. I will always be indebted to Micheners for the time they gave me.

Stephen Blackburn
Hollywood, California
August 26, 2000

1

webs center

all the webs that cover all the cracks on all the rough green shingles on all the sides of his house enchant him they are not the clean neat pretty webs he sees in big slick picture magazines all sharpfocused with sun bright through diamonds of dew

the soft fuzzy white cobwebs on his house feel kind of like cotton candy to wipe off his hands but they taste like dust and he bets they are old as once upon a time its like having a haunted house only on the outside he likes to peer into the deep holes at the dark center of these endless webs you can never see inside them

he has tried

it almost always seems like the spiders arent at home but he knows they might be

that is enough

inside his house mommy stands at the ironing board pretty with her smile and he likes to rub his hands over her big watermelon tummy she has a big green glass gingerale bottle with a little corked dented silver sprinkler top that she shakes water on the cleanclothes with before she irons

for fun he knocks down a yellowjacket nest from the bushes in front of his house for the feeling their buzzing makes in him as he runs scaredycat clear to the edge of the street— but not in it—to try and get away

but they catch him buzzing madly stinging him so he howls

bloodymurder he runs crying inside from the yellowjackets she is nice to him and hugs him and puts stuff on his stings to make it stop hurting

   she knows how

   he likes to put his ear to her round hard tummy and try to hear his baby brother or maybe sister and watch mommy tug the white shirt around the different ways over the ironing board and the ironingboard sound the water makes in the bottle sloshing and the drops make crisp sprinkling on daddys freshly washed starched white shirts and the hiss and the damp warm smell of the iron sliding flatsmoothly on the clean white shirts the way the iron should are all things he likes

   he likes standing as the giant over the red ants who live in a hole in the gravel driveway bombing them with little rocks making blowup noises he spends a long time drooling spit bombs on them when they get hit they squirm over and all the slow ants start running very fast crashbumping into one another

     how come they make no noise

        all of a sudden a stickery fire of whoknowshowmanylumpylittleredpincherbottombitersinhisunderwear he tears inside the screendoor slamming afraid of the hurting

    off his clothes ripping

          inside his cool airy house

   himself on mommys neatly made sunny white popcorn
               bedspread

flinging

crying

   she smoothes him with her humming hands making the pain softer with the cool greasy she calls oinkment smoothed on with her hands so that after he catches his breath he almost falls to sleep

   later he smells her get up and leave him going into the bathroom and hears her close the door there

   you dont often see the spiders who live in the cracks they

THE EXTINCTION OF RHINOS IN MEXICO

make him feel strange the way they dartle looking sort of like the tickly daddylonglegs
   but he knows they are different
   it isnt the same way like with the yellowjackets and the ants
some spiders have poison
   well he likes to play dead every day but he thinks he is not sure what it means only that nobody wants to be it really because then you arent pretendliking anymore
   mommy hasnt come out of the bathroom for a long time so he gets tired of waiting and he gets up and gets his robeon and goes looking for her
   he stands at the door to the bathroom still closed
   politefully he opens it and looks into

                                          mommy?

   mommys still there sitting on the potty
   at first he thinks shes having a hard time pooping
   then he sees whatintheworld whomadesuchamess on the floor in the tub on the wall smells and splashes of red all over the place
   he knows blood from when he cuts his finger or scrapes his knee sometimes but theres too much of it here for it to be that like some bad boy took his paintbrush and painted where he knows hes been told not to
   she talks to him quietly so maybe its not scary
   please go next door brad and bring missus crowell
   when he tells missus crowell and about the bathroom she swallows funny and walks a lot faster than him to his house
   missus crowell forgets and hooks the screendoor behind her so now he cant get in
   susans mommy and daddy from across the street get his clothes from inside and holding his hands walk him looking both ways across the street inside to their house and they leave him alone in their bathroom different than his bathroom

but he dresses all by himself forgetting his robeon because they call him

    theres strawberry cake and milk waiting for you brad
    susan gets some too

    somedays he plays with susan she always sucks her thumb so her fingers are always drooly and red like a tbone steak when daddy lies it on the little stone grill over the orangehot charcoals out in the backyard and they make her wear leather gloves a lot of times so she will stop

    but she doesnt

    by the time he pushes open the screendoor on susans porch they tell him daddy came home from work all ready and took mommy to the hospital where she will be fine and youre supposed to wait here

    he sits and watches across the street other grownups going in and going out of his house

    he hears susans mommy and daddy inside susans house on the telephone and he doesnt know all the words but hes pretty sure now he is not going to get a baby brother or maybe sister

    susan on her porch beside him is sucking on half a lemon that is making her teeth bleed

    she gets tired and goes away inside her house

    he stays sitting on their porch watching his house across the street in the late afternoon sunlight and he wonders if its time for clutchcargo or spaceangel on tv

    watching the shadows creep stretchy fingers of night upover his sunny house the boy figures it must be like being caught deep down in the dark spider holes wrapped tight up in webs so squeezing you cannot ever budge all the time or everagain catch your breaths or neverever play or ever after have on your tongue first the green taste of a lime lifesaver and then the red flavor of a cherry one

    so now the little boy never looks for spiders and this way he will never tease them and get bit by them

THE EXTINCTION OF RHINOS IN MEXICO

so it will never happen to him
but he can never forget they are there somewhere inside the dark deep holes of the cobwebs on the outside of his sunny cool and breezy house where mommy inside is sprinkling and ironing clothes

2

The Extinction of Rhinos in Mexico

I am very poor, aren't I? Some mornings when I wake up in my little house I am surprised and don't recognize it, even though I myself collected the limbs and lumber scraps and cardboard, without any help from my husband Justino at all, unless you call bossing a help. He has handsome green eyes to go with his brown skin and with his hair, which after these many years remains black. In reality, those green eyes are why I fell for him when both of us were young.

With these ugly brown hands of mine I used an old nail to make holes along the edges of the cardboard and some plastic garbage bags so I could fasten them all to the posts using pieces of wire I found and some of the thread with which I embroider tortilla napkins. Sometimes people will buy those napkins from me outside the tortilleria or at the Tuesday plazita. The walls finished, I then took my own hardearned pesos and centavos down into the pueblo to buy a few sections of lámina, the plastic type, furrowed like a field, which I carried up here one at a time. Using that I constructed the roof, which works well, though for some time now it has had several broken places. Not too many. Certainly I would have built the roof higher were it possible, but you know, the tree limbs I have for posts only grew so long. It's fine for me, as I am short, but my teenage son Esteban complains of bumping his head on the ceiling whenever he stops by to see if I have anything for him to eat or

THE EXTINCTION OF RHINOS IN MEXICO

spend. Esteban and his two older brothers have eyes like mine, like obsidian, so they have to romance girls justly. Those times when Esteban or his father Justino come to spend a night, I hide a little something for myself to eat, but I let them sleep in the bigger room, the one where the lámina has no leaks and two lengths of board serve as roof beams. My other two grown sons I never see, which is a blessing.

Over time I have formed this bramble fence around my house by piling brush that dries into a good tangle. It's been necessary to wire it in a few places. The gate is tricky: look, you work it by lifting it off its hinges, and at night I wire it shut for safety. It's a good fence that keeps my puppy and chicken from straying. Still, I must tie my little goat to a stake to keep her from enjoying herself in the patch where I grow some mint, some marjoram, a corn plant, nopal cactus, a few roses, even some manzanilla for tea which I make if a sister in law or my cousin or my comadre happen to visit.

Look, Justino is my true husband, is that clear? I am not one of the shameless, living in sin like several women I could name, but won't. Because in reality many around here cannot afford the expense of even a simple church ceremony. But Justino and I, we scraped up the money to be married by a priest in the colonia San Antonio church twenty three years ago this coming June. Our wedding took place just as a thunderstorm spread over the afternoon like a dark owl swooping down from the high ridges above the old reservoir. However, by the time we walked out the doors of the church, man and wife, the downpour had already spent itself. Dripping tatters of clouds still hung low and gray, like an exhausted threat, their cold tears gushing down the streets, and steam was floating up like spirits from the hot cobblestones in the crystal sunlight. The tempest had swept away the summer heat, leaving us a clean, lovely coolness.

For my bridal gift, he gave me a delicate silver rosary, which I kept with me night and day. My present to my husband Justino was the hat that he wears to this day. It has a flat crown and the two small tassels at the back of the broad brim. It is of the dense, flexible straw from Michoacán, very durable. I tell you, I spent some money on that hat, but it was worth it to see how handsome he looked in it, and how proud. When I gave it to him he favored me with a smile, blessed as he was with strong, straight teeth. During our honeymoon my beloved brought stars to me by means of a brass tube with special glass lenses. That gadget had been handed down in his family for eight generations.

Soon after we were married we rented a decent little place and presently I had the signs that I would soon be carrying a little burden. One day not long after I told Justino, he cradled the brass tube for stars and stepped aboard a Yellow Arrow bus, riding it for so many hours, all the way to Mexico, the Federal District. Have you ever looked through a such a brass tube? I was sorry to see the thing go. In the capital, he used it to borrow money from the national pawn shop, the one run by the Church since before the revolutions.

With the loan he set down the first payment on a used automobile which he painted the turquoise green of the local taxis. Driving long hours each day, Justino earned a good amount. We were doing well, starting to pay off the loan and even buying some things for when the baby came. While we had some cash, I urged him to pay the fee for joining the taxi syndicate and for the taxes on the waiting stations along the zócalo, but you see, in those days there was no hospital here. All I needed was his sisters or a midwife or two, but Justino wouldn't hear of it. He had been to school and believed in modern ways, so he spent the money instead to send me to the clinic in Querétaro to have our first child, baptized as Carlos Maria. Justino told me not to worry about the drivers union, that he had a friend at the town hall.

There's a hole in the roof of this little room where I sleep and my casita has no toilet, but not far from here is a thicket, near the dusty soccer fields, so I make sure to visit there each dawn and dusk when there's nobody about. My room is not much bigger than this vivid wool blanket I sleep on, is it? I spread the blanket over straw which softens the swept, hard dirt floor. You can see how well I've smoothed this by carefully pulling out all the sharp rocks. One day soon I will repair that hole in the roof, but look, it's not worth the pain now because the raining season doesn't come until May or June, and well, there is no electricity in this colonia, so at night when there is only the noise of the stray dogs fighting near the slaughterhouse and the lonesome complaints of the big trucks grinding off along the road to Querétaro, I often light some copál, romero and resinous ocote wood in a tin can and lie on my back as the smoldering makes the air sweet and dreamy. It pleases me then to rest and gaze up at the bright little stars and recall the pretty colors I have seen during the day and the conversations I have had with people and think about the things I would do if I had a daughter to help me and the things I could teach her. That hole is like my television, you understand me?

When I realized for certain that I was pregnant again this last time, me, with two grown sons and one almost a man, I didn't leave my bed for three or four days. I was so sad that I was beginning to think someone had given me the evil eye. So when Isabela, a neighbor in the colonia, poked her head in one day to see what had passed with me, I sent her to bring the curandero.

So this curandero told me I was going to have a baby. I said to him I know that already, now what about the evil eye? Then he found a black woolly caterpillar under my pallet. He told me this meant someone didn't like me. He cooked a tea, which he had me drink while he crushed the caterpillar and put it in a plastic sack and then put that in the little pouch he wore slung over his shoulder.

—You will feel better by this night, he said.

For his services he charged me 4,000 pesos. Unfortunately, before he left he found that many black caterpillars were in my house.

—A lot of people don't like you, he said.
—Who?

I could not imagine. I mind my own business and gossip not very much.

—That I cannot say, he told me. But the signs are evident.

Well, I could not afford any more help. You don't want to owe such a man too much, so I paid him what I had, the 2,000 pesos and 170 centavos which I had been intending to use to buy tortillas and a votive candle or two. He let the rest go on credit.

Just as he had said, I felt better by that evening. Next morning I got rid of the other caterpillars myself.

I saw Justino even less as I swelled with his new child because he no longer wanted to have me. Or couldn't. Naturally he blamed me, saying that I was uglier than ever, that even the pulque no longer improved me, no matter how much of it he drank. It's true that I'm not so young anymore, a chaparrita shaped like a gourd, and I'm missing my share of teeth, but I bore him three sons, for all the good it's done any of us. Still, no matter what, I keep my silvering hair clean and wellbrushed, though its length runs down to my waist. I plait it neatly in back, holding it with a hair clasp of pretty plastic the color of the shiny green parrots I saw once in cages at the Tuesday plazita across from mounds of strawberries and mangos between a leather goods stand from León and the lady frying gorditas.

During the time I was with child, I sat brushing my hair one day, and my shoulder was aching, when presently a greenish bird flew past the door. It flew so rapidly that I could not tell you without a doubt if it was the same kind of perico I had seen in the market or not, but the more I thought about it the more I was certain that it was, and this one was free, wasn't it? No longer in a cage, and it was then that the thought came to me that the free green wings meant God made me pregnant to give me a girl. A girl who could brush my hair, a girl whose lovely black hair I could brush and braid, tying in blossoms and ribbons. With that thought I began to anticipate the day of arrival.

My belly had grown as big and heavy as a watermelon by that lucky day I went out searching for firewood to sell and ended up finding a rattlesnake. What happened was that I went out into the campo just after sunrise, as usual. Well sometimes I gather young cactus and shave the spines off and sell them for nopalitos, but many women from the campo do this. Better if it's the season for tunas, the sweet red pears that grow on the cactus. Those sell better, and you can sit almost anywhere in town and unload them all sooner or later. It works best if you display the fruits by making a little pyramid of them on a nice cloth tortilla napkin, like those I sew. Most days you can earn a few centavos and if nothing else, you can eat the red fruits yourself if they don't sell. You understand me?

That day, however, I was gathering firewood, because it was winter, and while winters on the high plains of Guanajuato are dry, the nights get cold enough, and many people in town need firewood. Firewood pays better than cactus. Whenever I could, I got dead branches still on the trees, for I couldn't bend down and had to kneel to get anything off the ground.

By midmorning I had my armload of wood, but still it remained necessary that I walk all that way down into town. That took until near siesta, because with my added burden I had to rest many times on the way down the steep cobbled road.

I walked through the center, past the police station and the town hall, past the zócalo with its ornate central bandstand and thick, square clipped trees. Right over in front of the high, narrowspired parish church is where Justino and I lost our luck.

On that particular day long ago, we needed a kilo of tortillas, so I had ventured out, carrying our second son, Alonso Jesús, swaddled in my rebozo, while Carlos, who had just started to walk, held my hand. You could hear the parish bells ringing and ringing. The men of the taxi syndicate had driven slowly down the hill to the square in solemn procession, their cars creeping along, decorated with flowers and images of the Virgin. They all parked in front of the great church, where they raised open the hoods of the taxis to have their car motors blessed by the priest. The curious North Americans who are always in the square began to gather to watch this pageant. As we passed through the square the priest was finishing, and I crossed myself, touching the silver rosary Justino had given me. But when all the taxis had been sprinkled with holy water, and the priest retired into the church, the drivers did not disperse. Instead, they stayed to talk. The more they talked, the louder and more forceful their voices grew.

My heart squeezed when I saw Justino's taxi crawl up the crowded street into the square. I wanted to warn him. He was still not licensed with the syndicate. Because of the traffic, he had no choice but to be funneled into the street in front of the parish church where all the syndicate drivers were waiting.

I stood there with my children in the middle of all those tall, mostly old and rich North Americans. I watched as all the drivers argued with Justino at once. Carlos recognized his papá and called to him, but Justino could not hear through all the voices. His passengers opened their doors and hurried away. I looked around and saw two police, but they were watching the event with amusement. Nevertheless, I went over to them.

—Please help the man, I said. He is my husband. These are our children.

THE EXTINCTION OF RHINOS IN MEXICO

—Patience, the young one told me. He is learning a lesson.
—No harm will come to him, the older one said.

The drivers made Justino get out of the car. The men rocked the car and then lifted it onto its side, breaking the mirror on the door. Justino looked on and I knew what it meant to him, and to me. I was afraid of what he might do next. I tried to go to him, but arms swept me back.

Another unlicensed taxi had the misfortune to wander into the square. For a little while the angry men forgot Justino as they began corralling that other unlucky taxi. Soon it was on its side as well, the owner negotiating. With everyone intent on the second cab, Justino saw his chance. He pushed on the roof of his taxi and it teetered, then bounced hard down onto the wheels. The noise made the syndicate drivers recall him. Justino jumped into the car and started to drive away, but they caught the machine, surging around it, so many of them that it could not even budge, though you could hear him gas the engine. This time they reached in, turned off the motor and pulled him out. Justino was pleading, in front of the whole town it seemed to me. Little Alonso began crying, and then Carlos. The men pushed the car all the way over this time, like a tortoise on its back. When the roof of the car crumpled, you could see Justino give up inside of himself. Two drivers came forward wanting to set the leaking gasoline on fire, but that is when the police stepped in. During the scattering of the crowd, I lost sight of Justino.

Even after things returned to normal, I stood there, my baby on my hip, my son clasping my hand in fear he could not comprehend. I stood there after all the taxi drivers went to work. I stood there after the tourists and retired North Americans lost interest and returned to their park benches, their newspapers and feeding the pigeons. I remained in front of the grand church and Justino's ruined car, too worried to even pray. After a while the boss of the police came out of the town hall on the other side of the square to supervise the tow truck that came. The boss was handsome in his uniform, like a television star. He smiled and chatted with the North Americans as they would stroll past. The truck driver and several policemen lifted the wreck and shoved it right side up. They hitched the crane to the bumper of Justino's taxi and then the truck drove away with it.

Ah well, that was some years ago. I was speaking of more recent events. Look, tourists don't buy much firewood, so I continued alone down past the zócalo, carrying my armload door to door in the colonia San Juan de Dios, where live some local people who have some prosperous little businesses. In fact, I sold my entire bundle to Antonio, the old carpenter with his shop on Calle Beneficencia, just as he was locking up. He gave me 6,000 pesos for the load. Now there's a gentleman.

Unfortunately, right around the corner, I had the bad luck to run into some malditos. These boys were about the age of my son Esteban, and every bit as mean. On the street called Indio Triste they cornered me, taunting.

—You all go on out of here, I said, waving them away.

Oh they laughed, for how could I frighten them in my condition? Very rapidly they were grabbing me and pawing my apron pocket, tearing it as they stole the pesos I had just earned. They threw me down and ran away before anyone could see what happened.

Well, I had to sit down in a doorway for some minutes with my hand on my forehead to shed a tear. I was shaking. Nuestra Señora but I was weary, yet at that time there was nothing at my house to eat, so what choice did I have? I started talking to some women at the permanent market. They gave me a coke to drink from a clear plastic bag with a straw. When I felt better, they said to me where a produce truck was leaving from the market. Thus I caught a ride in back of a rancho pickup out to the old train station, which stands surrounded by very tall, longleafed eucalyptus trees with smooth,

THE EXTINCTION OF RHINOS IN MEXICO

peeling bark. From there I picked my way in the gravel along the thick ties and iron rails of track, past the green cultivated fields and up into the rocky hills, searching for more wood.

I had found not so many sticks when I heard the rattle. I stood still as death until I could spy that he was coiled, waiting for me at the base of an ancient, dying cactus three times my height and twice my girth. Señor Viper had not yet gone into hibernation, but was already sluggish, so I dropped my sticks and with both hands grabbed up a rock as big as a your skull. With this I smashed Señor Viper's brains out and learned then, thanks be to God, that I had killed *Señora* Viper and what do you think? She was in my condition!

It took me the rest of the day to regress to my casita with my prize, but once home I skinned my snake and that night cooked it over a fire in my comal with a little bit of lard and some chilis I picked from a neighbor's garden in exchange for the skin and rattles. How tasty the meat was!

The next morning I didn't have far to go to sell the eggs of the viper. The brand new penitentiary is on the road into town. A guard there is the son of a woman that I know in the colonia San Antonio. I was able to sell the eggs for a good price to some inmates who know how to use them for making concoctions and potions which they sell to the guards.

As I left the prison, the world seemed suddenly to hold promise. You know, walking to the bus stop, I noticed some bugambilla growing up next to a train rail telephone pole beside the road. Now I never remembered seeing the plant before, and I had been there many times. Nevertheless, there it was, like a volcano of magenta. The sun seemed to show from inside the color, and it was as if my thirsty eyes were drinking in that color. That's the only way I know how to say it. I picked a small sprig of this happiness to put in my hair. With the thousands I had earned I might do all sorts of things.

I caught one of the thousandpeso buses down the steep cobbled road to town and paid a visit to the Virgin of Peace, better known as the Virgin of the Miracles. At her altar, in the smooth dimness beneath the high, immense ceiling of the sanctuary, I lit two candles to her. The thick, cool paving stone at her feet is worn to a hollow like a kind, open palm and varnished from the knees of her generations of supplicants. Do you know that her skin is the most beautiful cream color?

—A thousand thanks for your mercy and for this bounty, I said to her.

I dropped two thousandpeso coins through the slot of the box to assist my prayer that I would bear forth a daughter to share my joys and sorrows and to care for me in my old age. Listen, this Virgin is powerful. Once I had neither food nor money for many days and prayed to her for tortillas. No candles or offering, just my poor prayer. I swear it to you, perhaps two hours later she made me find one of the shiny new peso coins on the adoquín flagstones of Canal street near the corner of the zócalo. These new monies are odd, don't you think, that small copper surrounded by a ring of lightweight silver metal? Some say it is worth only one damned peso, but I know for a fact that it buys the same as a thousand. Look, you know how many other people should have seen that coin before me? So I had tortillas that day. Well if that's not a miracle, who can say what is?

I left the old Spanish church feeling joyous and wanting to share my good fortune. So I splurged and bought a jar of cajeta, you know, sweet burned milk. Of course, it is not truly burned, but is the gooey, caramelized milk of a goat. Then at the new central of the autobuses near the slaughterhouse, I caught a camión of the Silver Horseshoe line going to Dolores Hidalgo. It was tricky getting up into the bus with my round belly. It wasn't long until my day. As my own parents are dead, my intention was to visit Justino's family, bringing them the cajeta and discussing with them arrangements for the birthing.

The driver he was a good man, as you could see from the

THE EXTINCTION OF RHINOS IN MEXICO

fact that he had his boy working with him, and from the sequined picture of the Virgin of Guadalupe that he had posted above the green waving fringe that ran along the top of the windshield which had white markings on it near the door. Justino once explained to me those soap letters spell the major destinations. My husband can read, because when he was a boy he attended school for five complete years before he had to quit to help his father tend the fields.

As I stepped aboard this tidy bus, I noticed a blondie from the north, reading some magazine. I sat next to her, because I am curious, I admit it, and not too shy. She looked over and smiled as I sat down.

I smiled too, so I'm certain she noticed my missing teeth. But what made me a little ashamed was my grimy checkered rayon blouse and well, my red skirt is so old that you can't wash the stains from it anymore, and my knee socks are modest, but not at all fashionable. My shoes which are false leather have all but quit functioning. Even my apron was dirty. Ah, but the sandyhaired young woman was wearing old Levis with holes in them, and her hair resembled a bird nest, you know?

The autobus began, lurching out onto the boulevard, with its tall, dust powdered pine trees, and we went driving past a young mother holding one child by the hand and another tucked on her hip. In front of a truck repair shop, we eased over the bump of one of the topes, and I saw out my window two campesinos trudging into town, loaded with their wares, who paused to look at us and dream briefly of riding. As we accelerated noisily, smoke streaming from the tailpipe, the bus driver's son worked his way back to me, paper money crisply folded between each of his fingers on one hand. I told him my destination. It cost me 3,000 pesos, 75 centavos. I handed him the coins and he gave me change and the thin paper ticket and then he ambled and swayed with the vehicle, back up front to sit by the door across from his father the driver. They had a radio and it was playing a friendly accordion polka.

—Güera, you like to read? I asked the North American. She looked at me. Being a blonde, her eyes should be blue or green, but I saw they were brown.

—Forgive me, my Spanish is not very good, she said. Another time, for a favor?

Her pronunciation was poor, but I wanted to talk, so I understood her.

—Ay, but your Spanish is excellent, I told her more slowly. Listen, girl, what I said was, you like to read, true?

She got it that time and looked at her magazine, which had a yellowgold border and a picture of some bird on the cover. I saw it was not a fashion magazine nor cartoon novela.

—Yes, said the güera. This magazine is called—she pronounced it carefully—"Geográfica Nacional."

—Ah. How many children have you?

She smiled at me the way nuns do.

—I have no children.

—I'm very sorry. You were sick?

—No, she said, still smiling. Already I am not married. I am not prepared for children. How many do you have?

—Three and now this one.

I was embarrassed for her. You know, by her age my first two were almost fully grown. Not prepared? Perhaps for some reason she could not attract a man.

We rode a while without speaking. Our camión made several more stops. She was looking out her window at the countryside more than she was reading her magazine. Looking sideways I could see it had color pictures throughout. She noticed me.

—Would it please you to look at this? she asked.

I grinned and she handed it to me. The pages were very

THE EXTINCTION OF RHINOS IN MEXICO

slick and had a strangely new fragrance. I touched the smooth little black marks.

—It's in English? I asked.

—Yes. Can you read English?

—Just a little, I said. (Although you and I know I can't even read Spanish.)

Carefully turning the pages, I saw wondrous, vivid pictures of tiny cows and monkeys and birds and some strange little people with yellowed skin and slanted eyes, and later some pictures of odd little gray creatures with two curved horns rising from their snouts. Have you ever seen such a thing?

She pointed to the small strangehorned animals in the magazine. The horns both curved upwards instead of out to the sides.

—That is a . . . (she paged through a small book) a rinoceronte.

—I have never seen one.

—Oh, they live far away. In Africa.

—Ah. I nodded. (Perhaps it also was north.)

—They are a . . . (again she looked in her little book) endangered species.

—Yes. What does that signify?

—They will become extinct if people do not stop killing them.

—Extinct?

—No more left. Totally all dead.

—Why?

—Because people kill them for the horns. To make a powder with the horns.

—For a remedy?

—Well, not in reality. There are men who believe that it increases their potency.

Both of us looked at my belly. I covered my mouth with my hand as we shared a laugh.

The bus went along and then came to a stop at a vineyard. The güera got up and said that this was her stop. I handed the magazine back to her.

—Until then, she said. She pronounced it in the shortened local manner. I smiled.

—See, your Spanish improves already. May you go well.

She smiled and nodded. From her expression I don't think she had understood all of what I said. But just as she was at the door, she stopped and walked back to give to me the magazine as a present. I remember now that she smelled as vanilla.

That bus rumbled on along the rolling pavement in the warm winter sun, the mountains of Guanajuato in the far mist of the western horizon. We drove past haciendas and scattered villages and rocky plowed ejidos outlined by generations of low, snaking stone fences and children playing outside plastered cinder block country buildings with walls decorated by announcements freshly painted in rainbow colors. We were making many stops for women carrying brightly checkered woven plastic shopping bags with handles, and dusty, sunbaked men stepped aboard, only a few with the mustaches these days, most of them no more than scarecrows or phantoms with bright eyes, wearing tired clothes with sweated and wornout straw hats.

Presently a young woman about the age of my last son boarded the bus. She was wearing handsome spiked heels, as even the nice girls do in these times. The way she was dressed up and lip-penciled, I thought: *She is a nice girl going into town, into Dolores to shop or visit her grandmother and go to Mass, or perhaps going for a job which pays well*. Her happiness brightened the bus, and then behind her came her father, likewise festive and bounding up the steps, wearing a finequality straw hat from Michoacán.

No, not her father.

THE EXTINCTION OF RHINOS IN MEXICO

His eyes changed when he saw me, but he is a man, so he did not flinch when his woman, not knowing who I was, chose the seats right in front of me. They sat down side by side, Justino by the window, and the bus started again. My husband paid the boy for their fares and then leaned over to her and whispered something in her ear. Her head bowed for a moment. Even from where I sat I could smell the mezcal on his breath.

We rode for a few miles and then his woman let her right hand hang down over the seat rail, almost touching the floor. Before I realized what was occurring, she gave my ankle a vicious pinch.

That was all, nothing more, but well, I'm ashamed to tell you a fury overtook me. And so I yanked the black tresses of that woman in my callused fingers, and we got into it right there on the bus. Justino tried to push between us, but it took the driver hollering and his son threatening and then the hard braking to throw us apart.

The driver and his son ejected all three of us from the bus outside a solitary little grocery and drove away with a belch of black exhaust.

—Now look what you've done, Justino said.

—Her. It is her fault, I told him. My blouse was torn.

—You fat, toothless cow, is what his woman said to me.

—A mother. A decent mother, I said. Not a whore, like you.

—Who are you to call me that? He loves me.

She turned expectantly to my husband, who made a fist and hit my cheekbone. I staggered back. She slapped and pinched me. He boxed me in the ear and I sprawled into the dirt. I struggled to rise and he knocked me back down again. I tasted dirt and iron. He brought his shoe down on my back and I screamed. Then he and that bitch really yanked and tore at me. He kicked me and kicked me, even in my swollen belly. I swear his foot felt like a hammer with a machete blade on it. That's the only way I can say it.

I vomited and, well, I suppose I must have passed out, because next thing I knew I opened my eyes and saw the shattered jar of caramelized goat milk I had bought. Flies were skittling over the shards of glass, feasting on the sweet stickiness. That puta and Justino were nowhere to be seen.

I staggered to my feet, which took some time. You can imagine it was not easy, that far with child. I was drooling blood and another tooth, and found I was just about naked. Believe me, they had almost completely torn off my clothes and my hair was undone and tangled, my magenta bugambilla had disappeared somewhere in the wind. With my hands I shook my matted hair to at least remove some of the dirt.

I had many pains. My left brow and cheek, my lips, my back, between my legs. A sharp one, deep inside me. My anger grew with each new knifing hurt that made itself known to me.

Doing the best I could, I tried to reorder my hair. I realized then that my silver rosary was gone. What luck, I found it in the dust over by some old dog turds. The links of its delicate chain had been broken. I felt for my money. It was still there, hidden in my undergarments. Well, at least they had not robbed me. I gathered the rags of my clothes, and picked up the magazine, the gift of the güera. A few of the pages were creased, others torn. With my hand I tried to brush away the tiny gravels, but they left impressions in the slick paper.

I caught the next bus. They pass often on the road to Dolores.

The camión let me off at the dirt road, and I began a painful walk to the small country settlement, the rancho where my inlaws live.

By and by, from behind a willow along the trickling creek, Justino appeared. The mezcal had all been pissed out, I could see that from the guilt on his face. Already it was gnawing at his heart. I stopped and it hurt just to breathe. I stared at him for a moment. He said nothing, for what could be said? I was such a mess that he began crying, tears streaking the dust on his handsome dark face. I noticed then that he too had aged.

I led the way, limping and bleeding up the road to his father's house so his family would see. I wouldn't let him help me. Not even touch me. So Justino followed, his hat in hand.

Justino's mother had taken sick long ago when he was a boy and had gone to bed and never recovered. It fell to Justino's three older sisters, Ignacia, Ermelinda and Refugia to care for their mother and help their father raise Justino. That woman took 13 years to die. By the time the mother breathed her last, the daughters were too old to find husbands, so here they remained, living as they had lived their entire childless lives.

Several barking curs announced our arrival. Refugia stood up. Over the clothes line onto which she was clipping damp, clean shirts and pants she saw us straggling up the road. She ran into the stone house. By the time I made it inside the cactus fence, Ermelinda and Ignacia were coming out with their younger sister. Ignacia took one look at me, then turned to her brother and waited.

—I did this, he said.

Ermelinda went out to the fields. In a little while she returned with their father tramping across the furrows, over to where I stood. I was not caring to sit down just yet. The father of Justino is ancient but still has much force. The old man looked me over and turned on his son.

I watched the entire time Justino's father was beating him. His father is a painstaking man.

* * *

From the moment she was born after a day and a half of struggle, my little one cried. She had a lovely shock of black hair, but her precious face and eyes were squinched up all the time from hurt and crying. The poor thing was broken, her tiny hands clenched so tight, so tight, and one fragile leg twisted up behind her unnaturally. She already had suffered her lot on this earth. I thought that if only I could get her to relax her grip, she might know some serenity. To distract her, I told her tales from my magazine, the one given me by the güera.

—See these tiny yellow people with slanted eyes? They never grow any larger than this, I explained.

She needed so much care there was not even time to pray, so I tied my broken silver rosary around her wrist. It was necessary to pinch my nipple to dribble the milk into her tiny squalling mouth. Her need to swallow was all that interrupted her cries, which in reality were simply one long wail. Neighbors and relatives dropped by and brought food, but no one could stay. I was left alone with my daughter most of the time. It was not their fault. No one could stand it in the whole colonia. I think that such grief makes people think of their own lives too much. You understand me?

Each night I lay with her in my little room on my bed of straw in the incense of copál, romero and ocote and I showed her my stars through the hole in the roof, warming her with my own flesh.

—You take any star you want, I told my baby. Several even, if you wish.

By the furtive light of a little fire I showed her picture after picture and told to her a lifetime of stories from my magazine.

One moment she was crying, then she paused to take breath. And then the silence of the stars filled my home. My baby's tiny fists let go at last, seven days into this hard world.

THE EXTINCTION OF RHINOS IN MEXICO

With my pointing finger I stroked her miniature palms into relaxation and smoothed her aged brow to peace. Her tiny eyes opened as if for one good look at everything without the pain. I saw then clearly her eyes for the only and last time, and they were a lovely green. Even through my tears I couldn't stop telling her stories. I pointed at the magazine.

—Look, Esmeralda. Here is the rhinoceros. These are little rats with horns on their nose who run around and cause much grief for people. They are in danger of becoming extinct. If I see one, I will step on it for you. Honestly, I don't care if they die out altogether. Oh how I hope they do.

3

ORDEAL OF THE ARROW

First thing they did was lead the chosen away from the campfire and into the dark, where they blindfolded us like P.O.W.s. In the hot night they ran us blind down the hard arroyo trails that cut through mesquite and huisache and prickly pear. Ran us like a blindman's bluff version of crack the whip. With one hand I clutched the belt of the scout in front of me, while the guy behind me tugged at my belt until I thought my shorts were going to go half mast. As far as I knew, the rest of the ordeal candidates were getting the same treatment all across Camp Karankawa, so named in honor of the cannibals who once roamed the southern coast of Texas. I wished I was at home watching summer reruns.

"Duck your head," the gruff voice barked. "Tree branch."

"Ug," I said, and ducked, feeling the thorny limb rake my scalp. "Ug" was all they would let us say, making us sound like redskins in an old Hollywood Western. You know, Rock Hudson painted up to be the Noble Savage. We had the Vow of Silence on us for the whole weekend. It wasn't clear what, exactly, would happen if you violated the Silence. Public Humiliation, I imagined. Worse still, disgrace beneath the burning gaze of the chief.

Every one of us skinny, pimply kids in uniform held Camp Karankawa's Order of the Arrow chief in awe. The son of Major General Harlan Lee Bennett, hero of the Tet Offensive, Jack Bennett set records as a champion tight end for the Texas

THE EXTINCTION OF RHINOS IN MEXICO

Christian University Horned Frogs. He was magnificent, every inch the exemplar of tightended, unsmiling, savage Caucasian nobility. Earlier that evening, at the "tapping out" ceremony, to the hypnotic, thumping pulse of drums, he had stalked down each aisle, through each troop, studying the faces of the men and boys. One by one he singled out the secretly selected ordeal candidates—mysteriously recognizing them—and sent them in turn down to the fire. As he approached our row, flanked by four grim braves, you could see light and shadows from the great campfire dance like living war paint on Jack Bennett's face, and I couldn't help but secretly pray he would halt in front of me.

He had come down our troop's long row and stopped in front of Mark Struzick. Pride and jealousy skirmished within me as I watched Mark stand up solemnly. The chief honored my best friend by pounding him on the shoulder three times. Mark did not flinch. Escorted by two braves, he was sent down to join the circle of the chosen. Arms crossed, the chief and his fierce entourage slowly moved past our troop. You could smell the sweat, leather and Hai Karate aftershave. He was passing the rest of us by.

Then he and his biceps paused. So did my breathing. He turned and came back to stand tall and regal before me. Scarcely daring to look up, I beheld the shadowed, towering figure of Chief Jack in all his splendor: full length eaglefeathered headdress, a breastplate of long brass beads made from spent M-16 cartridges, breechcloth and breathtaking deerskin leggings that revealed his tanned, savage, All Southwest Conference tight end haunches.

With a nod he had gestured that I should rise, and my head swam with the primitive throbbing of the drums. My knees began quivering; I was mortified—what if I fainted? His solid muscles were cut and beautiful, his face chiseled with a stern, handsome honor that had made my stomach churn and my loins close ranks.

His sinewy left hand firmly grasped my shoulder, and then his right open palm pounded the bejeezus out of my shoulder, smacking it three times deliberately, in the ritual that meant you were better, and that those around you had admitted it. My shoulder burned, shattered I was certain, tears stung my eyes, but with the others gazing jealously at me in the firelight, I somehow stood strong and silent.

Last chosen from our troop had been a geeb with the unfortunate name Zeb Ferry. Zeb was a nice guy nobody wanted to be friends with. He had already earned more merit badges than any other boy in our troop, mainly because he didn't have any dates or sandlot football games or surfing to worry about. His whole life was clear and free to dedicate to racking up merit badges. Our troop had only been founded three years before, and it looked certain that he would be its first ever Eagle Scout ever. Meanwhile Mark and I had been plotting to bail. Too many sermons by the adult leaders. Too much selling: light bulbs, road flares, Scout O Rama tickets. Too much kid stuff. To be honest, the trustworthy-loyal-helpful bit had grown a little too corny. But Zeb was into it. He truly lived it. I honestly believe he had never lied, never swiped anything, had never done anything that might offend an adult.

The kerchief about my eyes slipped a little as we banked into a turn at a precarious dogtrot and started up an incline. My blindfold loosened enough that out the bottom of it I could glimpse the darting of flashlights through the brush. You could hear running feet on the packed earth, but no voices.

Finally they halted us. As soon as we stopped running, the humid lake air weighed down so that it was hard to catch your breath, and sweat trickled out of you in rivulets. Our blindfolds were torn off.

We found ourselves standing in a wide, weedy clearing in the thicket on some high ground. Before us, looming like an unholy cross between Steve Reeves and the Hulk, stood Studs

THE EXTINCTION OF RHINOS IN MEXICO

MacNeil. He was grinning at us, his fearsome teeth white in the starlight.

The scoutmasters and other grownup ordeal candidates didn't comprehend just who it was that had charge of us. But among the boys who had camped a summer there, Studs MacNeil was the boogie man. It wasn't just that he routinely failed kids trying for merit badges.

At Camp Karankawa there was a war game played called "Battle of the Flour." It was an old tradition there. The scouts at camp each particular week were divided into two armies, the Red and the Blue. Studs always refused to be assigned to the Red Army. Officers were chosen by election from the older scouts and counselors. Each boy was handed two fist sized paper sacks filled with sand and a little flour. At a signal, the battle commenced, and suddenly the air was filled with flying sacks of sand. If you were hit, you were judged killed or wounded, depending on where you were marked with flour. More sacks could be grabbed from each army's "ammo dump."

Once the sacks started flying, everything was yelling and chaos. I got killed right off the bat two years and wounded and captured this year. An improvement, but not an exercise likely to entice me to enlist for the real war.

Studs, however, got off to it. To his mind, the Red Army was always "Charlie," "VC," "gookville." He never settled for "wounding" anyone and never took prisoners. With his armload of sand sacks he would charge at each of his chosen victims and clobber the poor slob with a "saturation bombing."

That was who was in charge of us.

Studs spotted some candidate staring forlornly out into the darkness.

"Get back over here, maggot!"

Ashamed at being called down, Zeb Ferry scurried back

to the group, while everyone else was just glad Studs wasn't bellowing at them.

"Ug," Zeb croaked by way of apology.

"-Ly," piped another voice.

Studs wheeled around and glared at Zeb, who shook his head in frantic, speechless denial. Several people chuckled. I recognized the joker's voice and was glad. I located Mark in the darkness among the other scouts and slugged his arm to let him know I knew he was the one. Then Zeb found us, too, though we didn't really want him hanging around.

Chief Jack's minions assembled us in a circle. For hours, it seemed, they sermoned us on the lore of the Order, most of which was a Chingatchgook-goomiwhatchimacallit ripoff from *Last of the Mohicans*. Every time I felt myself being seduced, I would remember that Studs MacNeil owned my butt for the duration. How much of an honor was that?

What the powwow boiled down to was that we could expect a glorious weekend of grueling servitude. It was, of course, the ideal solution to camp budgetary shortfalls: maintenance performed by slave labor, inspired by elitist bushwah which brainwashed the prisoners into embracing this purgatory as a noble honor. Oh, and to make it an especially fine honor (cheaper), put the maggots on minimum rations.

"To prove your woodcraft," Chief Jack was saying, "and to demonstrate yourself deserving of membership in this solemn Brotherhood, you will each spend one night in the wilderness." He paused with dramatic flair, to let this sink in.

And then the other moccasin dropped.

"Tomorrow, at dawn, you must show evidence of your mastery of the Great Spirit's gift by presenting a coal from a fire of your own making."

I began to sweat even more. A fire. Made with what? Rubbing two sticks together? Flint and steel? Why hadn't they warned us so we could practice?

Studs MacNeil's henchmen distributed an army surplus

THE EXTINCTION OF RHINOS IN MEXICO

wool blanket to each candidate, which was a cruel jest in the swampy heat except you could use the blanket to flap away mosquitoes.

Then it dawned on me that our night in the big bad woods was going to be in this big crowd, together in this big clearing. It was like *Night of the Living Dead* with that many people shuffling around in the dark not talking.

Finally, they handed out matches. I gratefully took in my hand that beautiful, amazing, wondrous twig that is a standard issue strike anywhere kitchen match. And then realized that one was all I or any of us were going to get. One each. Uno. And no fair getting together with your friends and everybody starting one big fire. No more of that teamwork stuff. This was every scout for himself and devil take the hindmost.

Dang.

Now you may think it's no big deal to make a fire with a match as compared to flint and steel, but when you've got just one match, plenty can go wrong. Ever tried lighting a match under duress, with a shaky hand? In a breeze that suddenly rises up from nowhere? To top it off, a heavy dew had settled, dampening every blade of grass, every twig, every leaf.

They released us to our task and immediately every man and boy fell to scouring the dirt like armadillos, which are half blind, snatching up and hoarding every available piece of tinder like kids scrabbling after candy from a busted piñata. In nothing flat our overgrazing created a drastic twig shortage. The ground was raked down to dirt, yet I had scarcely scavenged a handful of tinder. Meanwhile, some of the adult candidates already had fires blazing.

I knelt like an acolyte over my modest stash of dead grass and twigs, stacking these artfully in the dirt. Then I realized I would need a surface for striking my match. Slight detail.

Somehow we had been deposited in the one area of Camp

Karankawa barren of its usual bounty of rocks and boulders. Glancing around for an alternative, I noticed a man lift one knee high, calling to mind a dog with a full bladder. Then he crisply drew his match up the under part of his pant leg. The match zipped along the taut material, flared into fire. Shortly thereafter the man possessed a respectable, crackling little flame.

Thus educated, I squinted at my lone match, my splinter of pine with a dab of dried chemical on the tip, then lifted my leg self consciously, hopefully, let her rip.

Nothing. Nada. Zilcho.

Time and time again I raked the match along my scout shorts.

Worse than nothing. As I peered at my match in the flickering light of infernal campfires jealously tended by their lucky dog owners, I realized that I had obliterated half my match head and damped the remainder with sweat from my thigh.

I glanced over at Mark. He was breathing life into a small, throbbing ember. I loathed him and cursed the Boy Scouts of America.

His own happy fate assured, Mark became a man of leisure, lounging on his army blanket, a sprig of grass between his teeth. Beginning to panic, I gesticulated until I got his attention. Then I pantomimed striking the match and followed it with a distressed shrug. Mark pulled back his fly to reveal his secret. He made a matchstriking stroke. Sure: strike it on the zipper!

In one swift stroke, success—in snapping off the fragile, sulfurous tip of my precious match.

I sucked air at the horror of it.

Panicked, my head began throbbing, pounding like a tomtom as I foresaw Chief Jack Bennett glowering at me the next morning, at which time I would become the only shameful ordeal candidate in history without a manly piece of charcoal to parade around as a trophy. My stomach went

THE EXTINCTION OF RHINOS IN MEXICO

hollow, something was stuck in my gullet, and tears welled thickly in my eyes. Full of bile, I glared across the camp at Studs MacNeil, holding *him* somehow responsible, but weariness and hunger soon deflated my hard ire to flaccid resignation.

Contemplative as he tended his small fire, Mark stole a look over at me. I could tell he was uneasy and I was shameless as a drowning man. I shrugged again, crocodile tears now mingling with the honest ones burning my eyes. He glanced around, then stealthily beckoned me. I knew what he had in mind. Sure, I was scared of being caught, but even more afraid of failing to measure up. But just as I started over to "borrow" a coal, Studs MacNeil suddenly stepped between us, facing down Mark, extinguishing my hopes.

"I'm gonna watch every move you make, turkey," he told Mark. "One itsy bitsy screwup and you're out, you're history."

"Ug, ug, ug, ug, ug," said Mark. He said it with a conviction that greatly offended Studs.

I knelt down on my blanket. With Mark under surveillance, I didn't stand a chance in hell of swiping a cinder from Mark's fire. I wished I *was* in hell; then I'd be sure to find all the coals I needed.

In the dark night I wandered like a hungry ghost over the knoll through the sleeping candidates, bracing myself for the disaster that would descend at dawn. I was getting too old for this kid stuff anyway, I told myself. Shoot, I was planning to quit the Scouts anyway—why not tonight? No time like the present. I began plotting my escape into the woods.

Late as it was, one crummy showoff still stoked his bonfire, by far the largest in the clearing. I lingered in the outskirts of the yellow light and gazed numbly at the raging pyre. He carelessly tossed another piece of precious wood on the conflagration. One stick must have been green, for it crackled and popped, snapping out sparks that made the men around it duck the fiery trajectories and chuckle nervously.

My blood raced as I glued my eyes to the end of the arc I had followed. Casually I edged toward a patch of cactus. Glanced down...

There it was, winking softly, intensely orange right down amid the prickly pear.

When no one was looking my way, I snatched up the treasure with my neckerchief, in the process burning a blister on my right index finger and filling the heel of my hand with dozens of minuscule cactus spines.

The Neanderthal Prometheus who nursed that first living cinder from a smoldering, lightning hewn tree in the depths of the Ice Age did not feel more relief than I did on that muggy Texas night. Lovingly I fed twigs and grasses to my infant ember, but the damp tinder only smoked and shriveled. Technically, I never did manage to produce an actual flame. Toward dawn, exhausted, I dozed fitfully between tagteam bouts with the mosquitoes and red ants.

Waking stiffly on the hard earth, I saw people already stirring in the gray light and wondered where I was. Then it came to me and I scrabbled in the dirt like a squirrel trying to locate a lost nut. A square knot and a double half hitch tightened in my gut—my ember had kept embering all night until there was scant left but a pathetic, tiny mound of gray ash! Grieving, I sifted through the ashes with fingers blistered and throbbing from the burn and prickled by cactus splinters.

And then I found it: oh, black nugget, more priceless to me at that moment than a diamond, my very own coal, roughly the size of an infant molar.

"Ordeal candidates, line up over here! Let's go! Move it!" The tender bellowing of Studs MacNeil was like hot coffee splashed in your face.

Mark found me and tapped my shoulder. I looked around

THE EXTINCTION OF RHINOS IN MEXICO

with a smile. I had the swagger of a veteran woodsman now and displayed my charcoal nub to him. He raised his eyebrows politely. Together we headed over toward the line of ordealers waiting to be judged by Studs, subject to review by Chief Jack.

On the way I spotted Zeb, adrift like a wraith. Heck, Zeb was the champion camper in our troop. I reckoned he'd made quite a blaze for himself, a huge fire, and that he must have a blackened *log* to offer up.

Or maybe not. I stopped him and the despair I read in his eyes spoke of tragedy. I motioned to him to show me where his fire was.

He took me to it. It was an admirable, no, perfect, architecture of twigs and leaves without any trace of any combustion. With jerky hand signals Zeb tried to explain what had happened, or had not happened, but mainly I saw the tear which trailed cleanly down his dirty cheek. I nudged Zeb in the ribs and nodded toward the smoking remains of Pyro Man's bonfire. Zeb shook his head. I understood and blushed in shame. Of course. Zeb couldn't cheat; it just wasn't in him. You could almost hear the drum roll as he turned away from me, facing the gauntlet of ordeal candidates.

It was time.

Zeb, who had been on track to become our troop's first Eagle Scout, was about to go down in flames for not having any flames. Zeb, the straight shooter, the squarest of the square scouts, squared his shoulders to meet his bitter destiny. Who knew how this might warp him? Boy Scouts was his life, and the University of Texas Tower was just a few hours' drive north.

I came mighty close to handing Zeb my charcoal. He deserved it more than I did, but wouldn't have accepted that route either, and frankly, I just couldn't quite bring myself to martyrdom on Zeb's behalf. What I did instead was this: Using my thumbnail I cracked my prize charcoal crumb in half. Well, more like thirds, since a portion of it crumbled to powder upon division. Then I made a show of rummaging around in Zeb's pile of tinder.

"Ug!" I declared. Zeb turned.

I held up an atom of charcoal. His eyes widened questioningly.

"Ug?"

I ugged encouragingly, pointing from the fragment to his barren fireplace. Well, we believe what we need to believe. He cradled the dark speck joyously, gratefully, and above all, carefully, as he scuttled over to the line.

That morning there were many who flaunted grotesquely large, long, burned sticks, and I despised them for their overendowment. Others proffered more modestly respectable charred stubs. Studs glared so intently at Mark and his charred stick that he scarcely noticed what a scrawny excuse for a coal I held in the palm of my hand.

It was different when he got to Zeb. While Studs was at odds with Mark, he despised weaklings like Zeb. With sarcastic fingers the Meanest Scout tweezered the mote of coal out of Zeb's proud, hopeful hand and scowled at it, his face contorting into an evil grin as he began a shake of his head that would inflict utter rejection.

Suddenly Jack Bennett stepped forward, shouldering Studs aside. Studs had no choice but to back off. The bronzed pseudochief examined Zeb's offering, then studied Zeb's earnest, fearful, completely forthright face.

That moment has become a tableau in my memory. Scarcely eight months later Jack Bennett was gone, dodging north to Canada. It was said that he lived alone out in the woods along a big river in a log cabin with no electricity. Along a different river, one that ran through Cambodia, Marine Lt. Zeb Ferry was killed. I forget exactly which year.

THE EXTINCTION OF RHINOS IN MEXICO

There was no battle. He was the only casualty of his unit that day.

But on a steamy Texas morning before those other things happened, Chief Jack nodded, and Zeb was saved.

4

Meat Caves

What had been bloody for days now sank into a grotto of oily black. Yet submerged layers of cerulean and cobalt blues stroked life up through the ivory blackness, and hints remained of the hidden, raging purples within. Deep swaths of alizarin crimson and flickers of titanium white and yellow combined to create stretching, tensile ligaments and sinewy, raw muscle. At last the image was coalescing, strong and definite. Nearly finished. To the clear, melancholy beauty of Klaus Nomi's woman voice singing the aria from *Samson and Delilah*, stalactites of gristle grew, and webs of muscle tissue twisted inside layers inside someplace dark inside some cavernous bardo.

Life is suffering.
The root of suffering is desire.
Desire can be overcome by right thought, right action . . .
Right.

Constance flicked her disposable lighter a dozen times, then threw the worthless thing across the room. *Couldn't even last one more day?* She matched the stub of a joint and sat back, opposite the widestretched canvas, on the floor with her back against the wall, to study the painted wholeness through curls of creamy, resinous smoke and slashes of winter sun, to bathe in sunlight and image, to sense where creation was headed and where it told her to go. *You know where.*

She sipped her coffee, viscous El Pico twice reheated

THE EXTINCTION OF RHINOS IN MEXICO

and then once more in the copper bottomed Revere saucepan that had been a wedding gift to her mother. The buzz from the smoke eased the pain in her lower back, and the comforting bitterness of the hot coffee on her tongue soothed her brain and the colors felt marvelous, and she drew a contentment of sorts, a nostalgia now that she would no longer have this, from the melanged scents of fresh gesso and linseed oil and the last stale swallows left forgotten and flat in the Black Label cans, and of the scattered, crippled tubes of paint, lidless turpentine and spilled ashtrays.

Finishing a painting wasn't like ending a sentence; no simple period—sometimes you thought you were done and then you'd get this rush as you realized a way to make the whole thing work even better, a way you'd never seen before, and off you went for who knows how long. But now as she sipped and smoked she saw that after days of working to track and manifest the alterations of her mind, of tapping into the Great Whatever, this last painting was approaching its final *you call that art you think calling it thats all it takes who would buy that ugly its crap nothing more worse than nothing an abomination no you cant say that you dont know shit an abomination youre not fit to pass judgment daddy shut up dont open your foul hole youll be sorry im sorry alright sorry that i ever spilled the seed that made you shut up daddy you dont know oh i know youre ridiculous here and pathetic in your squalid* mug of coffee clattered over and Constance heard the fragile crockery now instead of the arguing now.

She had heard something else as well. She listened again until she heard a cry, something beyond the opera.

Constance reached over to her dusty, paint scarred jam box and pressed the metal tab where the Stop button used to be. She listened and heard nothing. She hopped up and went out onto the freezing front screened-in porch. The ember of the sun extinguished just then and out in the world it was blowing three degrees above zero and fresh wet flakes swirled in the wind and the gray brooding sky was like some icy beast looming over the land intent on suffocating the world. Constance dreaded cold worse than being hungry. A homeless winter in the east Texas piney woods has a way of changing your attitude toward creature comforts. Cold was an old enemy, a malignant force held at bay. Nevertheless, she was dressed lightly and all her windows stood raised because old Mr. Himmelmann downstairs, who owned the house and lived on the ground floor with arthritis and bad circulation in his knotty, gnarled fingers and toes, kept the basement furnace dialed to Inferno, so that the heavy brass accordion radiators would brand you if you forgot and leaned back against one of them.

She looked down and out at the curb saw the old 1970s Caprice with mismatched beige and battleship gray panels. Mr. Himmelmann's friend Clint must be visiting. Not a soul to be seen anywhere up or down the block. No sound now but the muffled traffic along the snow quilted trafficway past Westport. Nothing but cold.

In her bedroom she reached under her bed and brought out the Garand M-1 she always kept there for protection. It had been her father's in the Navy and she sat on the edge of her bed and checked the eight round thirty-aught clip. The smell of gun oil and of the lemon oil on the polished walnut stock and the overall heft of the thing was so comforting that tears welled in her eyes. *This is my rifle, this is my gun.* Oiled and gleaming and ready for her any time. She opened her mouth wide a few times like an opera singer doing warmup exercises. *Just do it.* It amused her to think of her parents or somebody's parents, not hers, suing Nike for bombarding their unstable offspring with a message that pushed them over the edge.

There was the cry again. It wasn't fair to poor Mr. H. In Houston she'd found her roommate with her wrists opened, what a mess *you should have left her i didn't think and she was*

THE EXTINCTION OF RHINOS IN MEXICO

just a pup what did she know. Constance turned to listen to that cry and saw on the top of her chest of drawers the lovely huipil, neatly folded, the gift from Guatemala. She hadn't even known Dodge was back in town. She had been ready, willing and able, painting done or not, and then this, surprise at her own surprise and delight when she returned from paying all her bills off yesterday and found the package on the downstairs porch addressed to her and wrapped in Guatemalan newspaper. No postage. He had brought it by himself.

Leaving the rifle on the bed, she unfolded the peasant blouse and gazed on it, let her fingers glide over the brocade, let them absorb the dazzling purples and blues, and the red. In good light, sun light, the pigments would come alive; even now she could feel the colors physically massaging her brain. It was like all the warmth and brightness of spring had been captured in an alchemy of dyes and cotton threads.

Tonight's the opening.

With the huipil he'd left a card, thick cardboard with a tiny shaman he'd painted on it hexing her to come see the latest works of Peter Dodge. She lit a cigarette, stripped and studied herself in the mirror, artist looking at model. Felt her breasts and nipples, no unfamiliar lumps. Pinched her nipples. Breasts full but beginning to hang. Her face going too, a few years left maybe. Belly... *I'm starting to resemble a fertility goddess. Is that cellulite? Fuck! Do fertility goddesses have cellulite? Am I fertile at all anymore? Tonight's the opening. Shit, do not go too early, don't show up two hours ahead. Wait. Wait.* Her fingers grazed her trimmed pubic hairs and she pretended it was his hand, her breath coming quicker. Lying back on the bed, front sight of the M-1 barrel her digging into her shoulder, she wet her middle finger and spread her legs. A deft moist circling of her button and she was wet. She thought of Dodge, Peter Dodge, images came of him and her in a Guatemalan jungle, priest and priestess in nothing but magnificent jaguar robes, fucking atop a pyramid, now she was bound for sacrifice and naked, carried up — ·

Afterwards she felt glowy. *I wouldn't have lasted this long if I couldn't do that.* The day she learned it when she was twenty three she took the whole day off from work. *Do Guatemalans even have pyramids?* Gradually now the sadness began welling up again, lapping at her like a returning tide. *Oh, Peter Dodge why did you have to be nice now, just when it was easy? Love springs infernal. Or is it hope? Same difference.* An idea for a piece came to her whole and complete: *A wooden box, open at the top, painted sky blue on the outside, with innocent cottony clouds like you might see in a nursery. The inside floor of the box is dull black, and the walls are mirrors, four mirrors facing inward. In the center sits a bird's nest atop a tiny music box. In the nest lie three broken sparrow's egg shells. When the music box tune plays— a children's nursery song or something more classical?—the nest and its forever unborn eggs revolve gently, like a carousel. The top edge of one of the box sides isn't square, but a wavy cutaway angled down about 30 degrees, symbolizing infinity; functionally it allows the viewer to see inside the box from the side, seeing the nest and my three aborted babies multiplied in the mirrors in all directions out into infinity —*

She heard the cry again. This time she finally recognized it was Ulysses, Mr. Himmelmann's cat, calling to remind the old gentleman to unlatch the trapdoor window he had rigged for his pet. Ulysses had a low, throaty call that sounded to Constance more like "Arroo" than "Meow." *Poor gato must be freezing his paws off.*

She left the thirty-aught waiting on the bed and pulled on her sweats and out on the screened-in heard the scrape of the window latch downstairs. Mr. H welcoming Ulysses home, apologizing probably. She went back into her studio, and now, with the spell of creation ruptured, she saw the room plainly, in sharp focus, as she guessed Mr. H and the police would see it soon enough—spartan, with large oil and canvas laby-

THE EXTINCTION OF RHINOS IN MEXICO

rinths on every wall, the swivel draftsman stool on casters and the battered jam box the solitary furnishings in her studio forested with older finished canvases rolled and standing on end in the corners of this dark paneled diningroom which she had playfully christened Hard Cat Shoes Studio after she had moved in and found unexplained ancient cashews petrified where the still spreading spilled blackbrown caffeine on the paintspattered clear plastic dropcloth was threatening Mr. Himmelmann's hardwood floor, where she had only just a while ago been drinking coffee and smoking the last of her pot because her finger had landed on Kansas City instead of Toronto or San Diego. She always renamed her studio when she came to this next town. Maybe she should have spun a globe instead. *No. End of the line.*

She did not turn back on the beatup tape player. For the thousandth time she was on the verge of hurling it out the window, but now could not for the very same reason that had once driven her to want to destroy it: this inanimate object embodied a world of pain and pleasure for her, like some talisman. It was funny, once you'd made the decision, really made it, everything you touched summoned a fond sentiment, memories piling on memories until you were awash in your whole life at once, a sensory overload of past and present existing altogether simultaneously. The good with the bad. *Yeah, well fuck Yin and the Yang he rode in on.* Regrets, but at least there was no future now, no dread any longer.

The boom box, the cassette player, had been brand new when Lane Evans awarded it to her in Huntsville the day she hammered enough nails to satisfy the foreman so that he took her, a homeless runaway sleeping in a parking lot, made her part of the framing crew building an add-on to a Victorian house two blocks from where Sam Houston died. Lane was standing above her on rafters the first time she saw him, lanky, with the balance of a cat, his Jesus hair blazed up blonde in the sun. He flicked the coils of the air hammer hose around his hips simply as if it was his own tail and she heard him laugh. He had the best laugh.

The night he gave her the jam box Uncle Walt's Band had crooned softly from the speakers as by candlelight and incense and marijuana smoke she rolled clutching Lane, his damp skin the color of strong tea, his longmuscled body hot on top of her and hotly thick inside her own sweatslick flesh for their first time, his sunbleached hair loose and caressing her nipples taut and there was also the smell of a skunk in the hot Texas night, distant enough to smell pungently sweet.

Her hands blistered and became callused that summer, her arms ached and became muscled. What Lane didn't know about building a house wasn't worth knowing. The whole summer she worked side by side in the Texas sun with him. Ended each day drinking can after can of godawful icecold Texas Pride on the tailgate with the crew, joking, farting, talking shit, belching, admiring the work they got done and strawbossing Old Tommy as he finished hanging a door and checked it. *Tight as a 12 year old.* In the molasses nights Lane and Constance sometimes would fuck right at the work site. *We were always in half built spaces.*

A shiver went through her now—partly remembered heat and chained memory, partly anticipation of . . . an insidious gust of winter huffed through the open window. She remembered now that one night Lane came home after a "boys' night out" and he couldn't get hard for her. She nearly gagged with his soft penis in her mouth. It made her feel like she was molesting a little boy. She heaped scorn on him, but she felt to blame. When it happened again the next night she cried. He held her and told her it wasn't her fault, it was just Nature in all honesty letting him know they were through. You *didn't want permanence except in what you built with your own hands.* Soon after, Constance learned he had started balling the little waitress from the diner even though Constance knew that he couldn't stand the way she was always giggling and prattling.

THE EXTINCTION OF RHINOS IN MEXICO

Chatty Cathy.

Constance threw a torn shirt on the spilled coffee to soak it up. She kept her paint rags stuffed in her "Come Meet My Jesus" box. Not everybody had one of these. It was cardboard box constructed like a small suitcase; even had a plastic carrying handle. On the outside of it were the words and a staged photographic scene of Technicolor children smiling around the creamy Hollywood middleclass Jesus who sported perfect long hair and a sparse little beard, looking so insipid and saccharin that to actually meet such a Jesus would inspire the temptation to kick his ass. Her father would indulge the temptation, especially if he happened to catch Jesus peeing in the shower like the sailor she overheard him chuckling about one time when he was exchanging stories with some of his roughnecks, his a story from his Dubya Dubya Two Navy days, the world awash in killing and he felt obliged to thrash one of his own seamen for peeing in the shower, beat him while he was naked, which seemed to little Constance the scariest part of it *He was like Jesus How's that Because he turned the other cheek.* She remembered the sound of her father and the roughnecks laughing and Constance couldn't sleep that night at all. *What if Daddy finds out?*

Old Clint had given her the box. She didn't know his last name. He was Mr. Himmelmann's friend, bald, of indeterminate older age, though surely a full decade younger than Mr. H. Clint was buttugly, tall for a gnome though, his hornrim glasses well propped by a beak stuffed with irongray bristles. He was stout and bowlegged and *so what youre fat wait til you get jowls i didnt mean anything you never do you stupid fat ungrateful please dont i will try to be better what can i do tell me nothing too late you stink stop please daddy i came to you for help you ugly graceless mama tell him i am sorry i should hope so you know what you are young lady a sneak and i hate a sneak mama please now youll have to give it to some strangers to raise or kill it youll be a killer a murderer no daddy i dont know what to do mama youve made your bed havent you and now youve got to lie in it no sense crying i hate you both you foulbreathed crybaby slut no no no stop daddy stop doug stay out it mother doug honestly now youre going too far stay out it stop this stop it both of you dont doug stop slamming her head against the wall well look at me mother bleeding look where your daughter bit a hole out of my goddamn chest* not just a friend but the best buddy of old Mr. H downstairs, the only buddy so far as Constance had ever observed.

She wanted to be kind, which she mainly accomplished by avoiding Clint, who repulsed her. She learned from Clint without wanting to that he had probably made thousands of Come Meet My Jesus boxes at the factory, along with all manner of less pious boxes, but of all the boxes, Come Meet My Jesus was his favorite.

Marco would have appreciated Come Meet My Jesus. Marco had been the most truthful of any man she'd been with, laid his cards on the table from the gitgo, was upfront about his enthrallment to the demimonde and he fucked men too or let them do him when the urge took him. She was hip and cool then and couldn't be fazed by any of it, somehow it made her cooler to be his then. A hairy man, he shaved his pubes and his anus and she found she enjoyed the sensation. He opened her in so many ways, taught her the great literature of the world and together they read aloud Cervantes and Swift, Melville and Marx, Blake and Borges, *Point Counterpoint* by Huxley, and *A Room of One's Own* that Virginia Woolf wrote, and also they took turns reading to each other Jean Genet, Nietzsche and the Marquis de Sade, and she began making real art then, flyers for garage bands destined to become legend, and Marco sent her to Jamaica to cover the World Reggae Fest for his upstart weekly and she came back saturated with salty caribbean colors which paradoxically found their way into the fabulous lithographs she created documenting the Houston netherworld of Urban Animal skaters and fuckups and brilliant artist flameouts and punk

THE EXTINCTION OF RHINOS IN MEXICO

bands backstage or vomiting on her livingroom floor from shooting up and she did it all but never would put a needle in her or let anyone. Yeah boy it would have tickled Marco to set up and shoot such a kitsch tableau as Come Meet My Jesus. But Marco was Houston, and after she had stumbled across the drying eight by tens hanging in the darkroom, artless but glamorously composed and lighted black and whites he'd taken of the runaway redheaded girl bowing before him, tiny eleven year old mouth engorged, Houston became dead as Huntsville to Constance. She walked in to an army recruiter's and they promised her a carpenter gig, so she signed her name, but at the swearing in before the U.S. flag she crossed her fingers behind her back.

She could not figure what on earth Come Meet My Jesus had been made for, what it was designed to hold (bibles?), but she wasn't about to ask Clint and run the risk of unleashing a rambling, unabridged history.

"It's a present," Clint had started hopefully when he gave it to her. "Ernie told me how you helped Ulysses."

When Constance had moved in, Ulysses was almost a year without his right rear paw, which he had caught in a rat trap set by Beatrice Decker, who owned and occupied the property next door to Mr. Himmelmann.

"I would've done the humane thing," Beatrice had instructed Constance on the steamy July morning when Constance had parked her U-Haul truck to inquire after the Apartment-For-Rent sign out front of the old redbrick house. A smiling, flying elephant on the porch had caught Constance's eye, its gray and pink plywood wings flapping on married eyehooks in the hot summer breeze.

Beatrice, hale and beef fed, had spoken to Constance over her picket fence and moat of tulips and geraniums. Never one to deprive another soul of her immense store of local history and neighborhood opinion, Beatrice had taken off her gardening gauntlets and proceeded to pigeonhole, analyze and dissect old Mr. Himmelmann and his crippled cat Ulysses. Thus Constance had also unavoidably learned ad infinitum ad nauseam about Beatrice getting her graying blonde hair done (once a month in short, pinched curls) and about Beatrice growing up in the large two story house where she lived to this day with her obese, disabled husband who spent the bulk of his life in the attic tinkering, adding ever more intricacies to his tiny Lionel train world, Beatrice said, though Constance found herself carried off by the notion the fat husband was truly a oncehandsomeprince turned into an ogre and held prisoner by . . . Beatrice had veered off on a tangent about how Mr. H and his odd buddy Clint had been union movie projectionists for decades until the contracts ran out with the big theater chains and the drive-ins so that nowadays they could only get part time work at a porno theater down in the River Quay, spelled with a Q but pronounced here as "key," and how Clint worked at a box factory and even how old Ernie Himmelmann, the son of an honesttogoodness Old World Guild gunsmith, mostly squandered his free time constructing those tacky plywood and paint eyesores dangling from his porch instead of keeping his hedge trimmed and the dandelions yanked and you know he probably wouldn't rent to Constance because he didn't get along with women since he got jilted years ago and a Negro had once robbed a house on this block so you couldn't be too careful and —

"I like them," Constance had cut in.

She had left the ambiguity dangling, enjoying the odd expression that clamped on Beatrice's plump, ruddy face. The mixed flock of fairytale flying elephants and flapping seagulls were precisely the quirk that charmed Constance, as she later told Mr. H. The old man had grinned at the revelation and blushed, tugging his stubbled chin with his knobby fingers.

He had rented her the upstairs apartment, the entire second floor for $400 a month. But his funk of sour cabbage and

THE EXTINCTION OF RHINOS IN MEXICO

bachelor underwear had a range of three yards, so Constance kept her distance. That part was easy: he was shy as a troll.

What Constance had not been able to bear from the first day was Mr. Himmelmann's cat Ulysses and his missing paw. Physical subtraction scared her.

She had averted her eyes whenever she saw the cat, because while he would gamely amble up the concrete steps to the porch, hitching that back leg up to keep it from hitting, the muscles used in running would inevitably bang the stump down.

"Arroo" he would holler, contorting the limb up, wracking his back around, perplexed by the pain. Constance had shunned him, yet couldn't bring herself to agree with Beatrice.

Constance had soon landed a job at the vast Nelson Atkins Museum of Art, with its entrance hall flanked by two rows of forty foot tall black marble columns. She worked in the bookstore, an undemanding job that allowed her to spend hours engrossed in studying the heavy, slick pages of expensive smelling, glossy art books. Sometimes she would sneak one of the books out to the high skylighted interior court built in 15th century Italianate style, where she often ate her sack lunch of an apple and M&Ms.

At night after a can of Spaghetti-Os she would paint, and on her days off she would paint and read or go to a movie or an art opening, and sometimes afterwards she would dream about the moviestar, or catch herself daydreaming about that painter she noticed by the cheese tray in one of the cheap rent brick warehouse galleries down in the Bottoms near the defunct stockyards where freight trains still lumbered by, slowly rumbling massive right outside the entrance. He was a shade too "the Bohemian," a bandana over his head, a scraggly beard. Bombastic. Handsome and charismatic and young. Earnest. Charming when he remembered to tone down the art/political rhetoric. She observed him, watched the way he dealt with people, especially women, gorgeous women, saw how they gravitated toward him. Constance felt the tug herself.

She had seen him again at several other openings, but they never met. Finally, at a fun sculpture show featuring dioramas and aquariums made from old tvs and dolls, after Constance tossed back four or five glasses of free white wine and shared a spliff with a couple of Art Institute kids out on the fire escape, she approached the painter as if she had the world by the shorthairs, introduced herself to Peter Dodge and gave him a firm Texan handshake. Then the artist ritual, the testing and name dropping. Dodge knew his Renaissance and Post Moderns. Weak on early Christian icons but a minor expert on Sumerian goatheaded gods. And he was a longtime Linda Montano fan. Drunk and too talkative, Constance prodded him to visit her studio to see some of her work. He smiled and said he would drop by some time. And then never did and could you die simply of loneliness, could you cry in the night until life flowed out of you with the tears? No, or she would have died ages ago and be dust by now. She was weary so weary and lonely that all she wanted was for it to stop. Just stop.

Tonight is the opening and we'll go from there.

She knew there was going to be sex, yearned for the connecting completing fullness of his stalk inside her, but first would come the wearisome struggle over condoms or testing and does he have an STD or HIV *does he even know hes not the type to care will scorn such carefulness why do you care if he can infect you its nothing to you anymore but worst of all will be the other how do you know therell be other women always is all i want now if theres going to be a now is a life partner alright a husband not just a fuck cant a man back me and i will back him so what if it sounds corny we will face the world together shoulder to shoulder and make art and love each other how what how if you wont even give him a chance why should i hes a man isnt he no wonder you fuck everything up dont you not me anyway why wait just cut out*

THE EXTINCTION OF RHINOS IN MEXICO

the middleman the middle time the good times only make the bad times worse how many times do i have to do this do i have to paint a painting make another object possession make myself presentable feed myself brush my teeth stuff myself with a tampoon fuck and get fucked and who would *fardels bear* —

Sunday mornings early, weather permitting, Constance always hiked to the Winchell's for coffee and a chocolate dipped donut (she fantasized occasionally about wallowing naked in chocolate like Ann-Margaret in *Tommy*), and then, before the museum opened, she would exhaust half a pack of filterless Camels, banging out letters to a small, no, tiny, roster of scattered friends and to galleries across the country and spending every dollar not used on rent, food or art supplies (including pot), toward the expense of having duplicate slides of her work printed for mailouts.

Most days when she clocked out from the bookstore, Constance liked to spend an hour or so wandering through the quiet, vast galleries, contemplating beauty and technique. Over time she explored the entire museum, and then began again.

Her favorite place of all was the Buddhist temple in the oriental collection. The central prize in the reconstituted temple was a 12th century, almost life sized statue of Avalokiteshvara, the hermaphrodite bodhisattva of compassion and wisdom, known in Tibet as Chenrazee, in China as Kuan Yin, who long before Jesus had declined the bliss of Nirvana, refusing the full benefits of enlightenment until all people had been helped to liberation. By that logic Kuan Yin must be out there still and would be for some time to come.

Kuan Yin in Kansas City was polychrome wood, carved into graceful life, herhis raiment a carved, flowing dhoti of royal green and red with gold brocade. A boy's chest. Heshe wore earrings and a necklace, herhis lengthy hair coiled in a topknot crown. What drew Constance back to the speciously acquired temple time after time was the gesture and the expression. She would sit for hours contemplating both.

Kuan Yin sat barefooted on a rustic divan, in the lovely posture known to art historians as *lalitasana*, "royal ease": right leg tucked up, right arm carelessly resting over the knee, grounded by the left leg, braced by the left hand and arm. Kuan Yin's smooth, round face was alive with perfect peace and compassion. Here was no wrathful GodTheFather or anemic Messiah, or faithless Casanova, but a gracious lover and powerful friend; a mentor with a wise, kind sense of humor.

Crosslegged on the marble floor, Constance would gaze up into that ancient face of youth, studying how *youve burned your bridges missy wait please you think you know so much well you know it all dont you* and when she was lucky she would absorb such serenity that it stilled the quarreling in her haunted head.

What Constance did that brought her the reward of Come Meet My Jesus: one afternoon, a few days after the first norther of her second October in Kansas City, Constance had walked home from her job to the papery applause of vermilion leaves, and coming up the steps to Mr. Himmelmann's house, she noticed tarnished crimson polka dot daubs on the concrete porch in front of the door.

With her key she let herself in to the hexagonal-tiled entry way at the foot of the carpeted stairs that led up to her place. Mr. Himmelmann's door was open and though she had lived upstairs for over a year, that was the first time she had seen inside his lair.

What she saw was the fresher polka dots leading inside to where Mr. H was down on the hardwood floor, on his hands and knees, painful as she knew that was for him.

"Come here, boy, oh come on kitty. Ulysses, please."

The cat had been wary, keeping his distance from Mr. H, hunched between the old man's upright oxygen tank and a squat, burnt sienna plastic Dr. Zaius Planet of the Apes coin bank. Yet his *arroos* were pleading. The right haunch twitched as Ulysses tried to hold his bloody stump off the floor.

Without a word, Constance had gone straight to Mr. Himmelmann's bathroom, cutting through the turquoise diningroom, doubletaking at the salmon colored kitchen, and rummaging in his medicine cabinet until she found alcohol and gauze and tape. She coaxed Ulysses and calmed him with talk while she bandaged and taped. She talked to Mr. H too, because she saw he was on the verge of crying.

Constance took the cat in a cab to a nearby veterinarian, a woman she had the luck to pick out of the Yellow Pages.

"In the long run," said the vet, who had closecropped hair, "Ulysses will probably be better off if I remove the remainder of his leg up to the hip."

The idea had startled Constance. She tasted bile. Yet when Constance saw the confident, gentle way the vet handled Ulysses, and the way he trusted the woman immediately, Constance had nodded. She made arrangements for the operation and the vet said it would be okay if the old man paid for it a little each month.

Only later, after Mr. H had been briefed and his stammering concern allayed, had Constance gone upstairs to retch. Only then did she recall Mr. Himmelmann's wild turquoise diningroom and surprising salmon colored kitchen. That made her smile.

Ulysses had come home to a hero's welcome, streamlined and bandaged. Constance cared for the cat during the many long nights he cried and struggled against hair raising hallucinations and nightmares induced by pain and heavy medication. Constance had cleaned the pus from the wound regularly, applied antibiotic cream and changed the bandages. She made sure Ulysses didn't squirm out of the ignominious, funnel shaped plastic collar he had to wear to keep him from gnawing out his stitches.

At last, after several weeks of being strictly spoiled, Ulysses the threelegged cat had mastered the new balance, cruising around better than ever. It was then that Clint had presented Constance with the box by way of thanks and celebration.

"Could I get you to come look at something?" Mr. H said to Constance the next day. "If you don't mind."

Intrigued, but a little wary, Constance had followed Mr. H down into his basement workshop, which bristled with the fine craft tools of his gunsmith father, including a wonderfully scarred and worn anvil.

"He brought that over from Germany himself," Mr. H told her.

He then showed Constance his assembly line system for jigsawing elephants, cardinals and seagulls, and then painting them and hanging them to dry. Rectangular blanks of eighth inch plywood stood stacked and ready. Brand new unopened pails of house paint sat waiting.

"Looks like you're going into major production," she said, marveling at the rows of B movies in silver cans gathering dust on shelves.

"I'm going to make a hundred of each and sell them at the swap 'n' shop at the 63rd Street Drive In."

"A hundred of each?"

"You know I used to be the projectionist there."

"Cool."

"Five nights a week."

She had smiled. "I always loved drive-ins when I was a girl. Those tinny sounding speakers you hooked on the window. I have this fond memory of falling asleep in the back of our station wagon while *The Sound of Music* was still going."

Mr. H. smiled then, too. "Oh yes, yes, I enjoyed seeing

THE EXTINCTION OF RHINOS IN MEXICO

the folks with their little tykes out playing. All the families." He quit talking and Constance saw him seeing back then. "You know I had weekends off, but a lot of times I'd go on out there anyway, just in case they needed a hand."

"What did you do during the rest of the year?"

"What do you mean?"

"I mean during the winter. When they shut down the drive-in."

"Oh, we never shut her down."

"What about when it snowed?"

"Had car heaters for people. Could plug 'em right in. We packed the place even with a foot of snow on the ground and more blowing in."

"Really!"

"People liked the 63rd Street. It's on high ground, on a hilltop. Beautiful sunsets from up there. They still do some business, though nothing like back during the 60s."

"I guess not."

"But here, young lady," and Mr. H peered at her over his bent wireframe glasses, "I need your counsel."

"What do you mean?"

Fervently the old man had brought out a new shape in unpainted blonde plywood. He handed it to Constance, breathing anxiously.

"What do you think?"

Constance held it up and considered it professionally. Its flippers waggled like wings.

"It's a dolphin alright."

"Think they'll sell?"

"Sure. People love dolphins." Once upon a time her father used to wake her before dawn those muggy mornings on the trips to Rockport to be his "fishing partner" when neither of her brothers could be dragged from their bunks, which was every time. She eagerly joined him and Mama in her robe and slippers would send them off with a thermos of hot coffee and precisely fixed sandwiches and in the boat Constance was enthralled to have Daddy show her how to bait the hooks and how to pet the dolphins that would sidle up bumping the boat with a playful thump sound. The rest of her childhood she longed for a dolphin instead of a horse. Years later, following the stint in the army, she landed in Corpus Christi and she remembered her childhood dolphins whenever she gazed out at the sparkling bay while laboring as a stagehand, unloading the big rigs at the Coliseum down on the bayfront. Her back was never quite the same after those couple of years, although since she quit stagehanding, she didn't have pain as constantly.

    She met Dennis in Corpus one night after she had played Puck in a pretty fair local production at the old Tower Theater before they tore it down. Afterwards the cast and crew had gone for beers and to play pool on the quarter tables at Chat's and she saw this Texas adonis playing shuffleboard and she introduced herself to Dennis after she had a few too many Lone Stars. He was six years younger than she was and worked shifts at the tall grain elevators out the port channel. He had a lovely, smooth naked body and she thought of him as her very own dolphin, *the dolphins are running*, he would say when he had a hardon, and she taught him how to really use it, used him, used that boy to fill the void until something better came along but karma is a funny thing because boy oh boy that boy could fuck and she got the dick addiction to where she had to have him and she didn't just want him for a while now but always because every time he would walk into the room he had a dolphin for her but the problem was that after a few months with her he had one for every other girl he met too. She came to the conclusion that it was wrong to debase the noble creature by associating it with her and Dennis' rutting. Tears, jealousy, anger, blah blah blah. It only irritated him, naturally, drove him from her, especially the anger, he couldn't fathom anger in a woman, he wanted a girl,

THE EXTINCTION OF RHINOS IN MEXICO

not a woman, was too young and vapid to tame, while she was hostage to her fear of loneliness so that he could always seduce her back to him whenever he happened to feel like sticking his cock in something. So she fled one day, abandoning her life there. Almost everything. Her mother used to sing a snippet from a song: *Kansas City here I come/Right back where I started from.* Constance thought: *No dolphins there.*

"Everybody loves dolphins," she repeated to Mr. H.

"That's what I thought. Only...."

He looked away from her. His shyness touched her.

"What, Mr. H?"

"The eyes have got to be right. I can't paint eyes. Never have been able to get them right."

It was true. His creatures all had something askew, lopsided, disturbingly *wacky* about the eyes.

So Constance had shown him some techniques of drafting and brushwork. She guided him through numerous practice eyes, until Mr. H had chuckled with delight.

"Well look at that. I think I've got the hang of it, I do. What do you think?"

At that moment she thought him dear. "You're a pro."

The snow the night of the opening fell thickly with thousands of compact flakes that refracted the street lights and the automobile headlights so that the world was bathed in a yellowgray glow and all the sounds of the city were muted except for the sirens and the diesel snowplows. The three man show was at Dodge's studio on the top floor of an old three story brick building on the Westside just a block up the hill from the place near the short trestle graffitied C/S, where the mojados would slip off the freight trains and stand in the mornings lined up along the wall of the convenience store waiting in the fumes of the gasoline pumps to be taken to work. Half a block up the hill was the place where you could eat authentic nopales and fideo.

Dodge shared his studio with Dane Godbold and Thomas Joyner, and they each had built themselves a dirty asymmetrical cubby hole to live in off on the north wall, living area given privacy by sheet rock wall with entrance by halfassed kitchen. Godbold was an angry young carpetlayer who came home to his condo one day to find his wife had deserted him for a corporate CPA. His life fell apart then, and along the descent he found he had a talent for oil painting. Now he always wore a leather cap and leather biker jacket and exclusively painted large, fascinating portraits of women slightly abstracted, distorted, always nude. Thomas was more an intellectual than a real artist, but quietly earnest in his humanist political renderings and in a constant debate with Dodge over whether or not video could be an art medium. Together the three young boulevardiers argued and painted and lived and created a happening alternative art scene based in the old hall overlooking the grand old Union Station, the hall where a generation of immigrant Swedes had danced and later the dancers were Mexican and now the dance hall was a vast studio space that Dodge sometimes rented out for raves to cover the rent. The old oak flooring was stained with decades of varnish and now oil paint, coffee and cigarette burns. The rows of tall windows along the east and west let light pour in even at night and the spacious fourteen foot ceiling made the place seem like an art cathedral with Peter Dodge its manic iconoclastic pagan high priest, sage smudge burning, *Fight the Power* blasting as he stood on the stage, a performer painting Mayan images in tar and gold flake and oil colors troweled on sometimes dense as the rain forest, visions gathered and stored on his yearly quests to Guatemala.

    Dodge was genuinely pleased when he saw Constance across the crowd. He broke away from a cluster of badboy sculptors from the Institute and came over to her, took both her stained hands in his own stained ones.

    "You grace me, Constance."

    "I'm glad you realize what you're getting." *A suicidal old*

THE EXTINCTION OF RHINOS IN MEXICO

woman of 35.

"Oh, without a doubt. You've got an uncommon and I'd say unerring sensibility."

"You're not so whitebread yourself."

They smiled at each other. She took off her coat, an old brown thing of her mother's, from the 1940s, and he saw she was wearing the huipil he had given her, even though it was too cold for such a light blouse.

"Que hermosa," he beamed.

"Gracias."

He gave a little bow. "Para servirle." He drew closer. "Believe me, it's really only a very modest token to show you how much you were on my mind three thousand miles south in a Mayan Indian's choza."

"Really?"

"Surprised the heck out me, frankly."

"I adore it. And gosh, look at you, turned all brown from the sun."

"Brown as a gabacho can get."

Halfway through the evening, after a couple of hours being jostled and nudged against him by the hot, smokey crowd, Constance let herself be drawn away to the privacy of his chilly room, an angular, cluttered warren smelling of burnt sage and marijuana, farctate with taxidermy, amulets, ratty pelts and Native American trinkets.

"As cold as it is in here now," he said, "it's the complete other extreme in the summer."

"You like extremes."

"Oh, I'm a manic depressive so I feel right at home in this building."

They laughed.

"It's so hot in August," he said, lighting a Marlboro and sharing it with her, "that I climb up the ladder onto the roof to sleep naked under the stars."

She realized he was one of those types who makes cigarette smoking a subtle performance, sexier than all getout.

"The roof's tar, right, and soft from the sun for half the night. It's a fabulous view. And windy as the devil." Constance noticed he punctuated with his hands.

"Windy?"

"Kansas City's a high point above a major body of water."

"The Missouri River."

"Precisely. So geographically it's a crux where weather patterns collide. Although strangely, tornados veer away. Something about the shape of the land, I'm told."

"But it is windy."

"I anchor my sheets with old stage weights."

"Sounds romantic."

"Oh, very. Extremely. I'd show you now but we might hit an icy patch up there and slide right off." His hands illustrated. "Involuntary Lovers' Leap."

"Lovers' Slip."

"Lovers sleep."

"Lovers."

She looked him deep in his brown eyes. They kissed, first kiss, savoring. Then separated, eyes scanning affectionately. Constance could hear the art crowd nattering on the other side of the wall, and the muffled music and Dane Godbold holding court, ranting about some issue, no doubt a can of Old Milwaukee in one hand, a filched cigarette in the gesticulating other. She and Dodge shared a joint that was dangerously smooth and sweet, and he showed her his sketchbook from the Guatemala trip and the weed was making her head slowly contract and expand simultaneously as they debated about Joseph Beuys and tattoo art and all the Germans in Guatemala and hydroponically grown *Psilocybe Mexicana* (oh magic bare head!) and tales about themselves and then Peter Dodge was awkwardly relating to her about the priest who had sodomized him as a young teen, and so she stroked his hair out of his eyes, caressed his whiskers and told him about the tv repairman who had felt her up when she was eight, and just when it was getting too quiet in there and was on the verge of getting too icky they each erupted overlapping each other with crazy, daring ideas for public art, wild ideas that would put them on the map. They kissed again, tenderly, longer and then launched into a playful brainstorm of installation possibilities, related to graffiti somehow, but different, so people couldn't just dismiss it right off, couldn't help but see art that would change them, and she could see in his eyes that Peter Dodge got it, he was kindred. Constance felt a hotness in her head that was umbilicaled to her womb.

"I have to pee." The seat was freezing, so she squatted above it. The north wind rattled the window and huffed frigid air at her through cracks in the mortar. Her teeth chattered.

When she returned, Dodge left to grab them more wine.

Constance sat very still, scarcely breathing. Oh, she had thought she was done. But she sensed the opening now, this fresh wormhole of chance, her past intersecting with a stranger's at this present unforeseen point, and she saw the myriad ways it would go the many years of their future history together spiralling out from here now, his with hers; their own fucking, their own joys and tears, children of their loins, all their own together secrets and disappointments carried with them to the wonder of their graves.

He could ask me to do anything tonight. There's a chance he's worth it, isn't there? How many tears have I cried on the altar of my pride and cowardice? I'm so weary.

Then suddenly she was rooting through his stuff, expertly unearthed five recent love letters from three different women, some used silk panties and a photo of a breathtaking African American woman, topless. Gazing at the image of the woman, Constance felt a knot in her stomach. *Damn*, I'd *like to fuck* her.

She hurried out, left by the fire escape, taking the icy iron stairs fast, too fast, so that once she very nearly took the leap by herself.

"Constance!"

Was in her studio again now surrounded by caves of meat, standing wobbly on the draftsman stool in the middle of the night, rope around the chandelier and scratchy around her neck. A noose tied very short. She'd decided the mess from the thirty-aught would be rude to Mr. H. Her damn period had started and she was fighting waves of cramping and she was out of tampax but it didn't matter nothing mattered —

"Constance! Constance!" And fucking Clint was banging on her door.

"Go away!"

"Ernie. It's Ernie!"

She undid the rope, climbed down and yanked open door to find Clint dancing like a kid desperate to pee and nowhere to go.

"You better come help Ernie. Please hurry!"

Downstairs in his livingroom, Constance saw it was bad. Mr. H was slouched on the couch next to his tall tank of oxygen, but he didn't have the breather on and his head was back and his mouth open, his face bluish. "Prussian blue" crossed her mind.

"Mr. H! Mr. Himmelmann!" She shook him. "Ernie! Hey, Ernie, can you hear me?"

Oh God, what are you supposed to do now? It was years since she had taken CPR.

She felt for pulse. Nothing in his wrist. *Life is suffering.*

She pressed two fingers on the loose skin of his neck, finding the carotid. Something there, but only a murmur.

"He was sitting there laughing. We hadn't laughed like that in I don't know how long." *The root of suffering is desire.*

She brusquely ordered Clint to the phone in Mr. Himmelmann's bedroom to call 911 so she could get him out of the way so she could think. It didn't help that Ulysses sat there staring at her, wide eyed.

Desire can be overcome by right thought, right action. Constance wrestled the old man's bulk into a prone position on the couch. Listened for breathing: none. Tilted his head back, exposing the coarse white hairs in his nostrils. His stubble prickled her lips as she planted her open mouth over his already cooling one, and she heard the sirens begin as she alternated between breaths and compressions *Life is suffering. Life is suffering. Life is suffering.*

The sirens swelled, monstrous Sirens calling outside the house, and Ulysses was made frantic by the shriek. He shot through the trapdoor in the window that Mr. H had made for him, and was gone.

Silly roadrunners stood at their posts in the freezing red lights flashing in the front yard and the wind blew their frantic legs awhirl and they never got anywhere. The flying elephants and red cardinals and dolphins flapped goodbye as the medical technicians carted Ernst Himmelmann away. Up at the window of Beatrice's attic, the curtains parted briefly, then fell closed again.

Constance didn't feel any of it until half an hour after the EMS left. He had lain there so still and ugly. *We are all meat in the end meat* yet once he had been his mother's pink, smooth baby. Beloved. And she loved him *love what do you know about love youre a slut a tramp a no listen daddy he says he will help me not marry you of course you are so stupid and ugly* and abruptly she went shaky and sank to her knees, nauseated. *Stop please stop.*

She felt an overpowering urge to see Peter Dodge. She listened to the phone ring endlessly. No answering machine of course. Neither had she. He was asleep or gone or the music was too loud or he was fucking one of his groupies. *God damn not having a car.* Too cold and far to walk. Too late for a bus. Too scared and old to thumb. *God damn getting old.* She looked at the rope hanging in her studio and suddenly felt embarrassed. She dragged on her army jacket and went out.

Shatterings of sleet pecked her cheeks and she inhaled the night, coughing, but for once grateful for the hardness of the arctic air.

Hands stuffed deep in her jacket pockets, hood pulled up, she settled for walking down to the old allnight diner at the end of the street, where inside at the counter she ordered a bottomless cup of bad coffee and lit the first of many cigarettes. Dana, the tall, sweet tranny waitress, let her sit as long as she felt like and made an outoftowner businessman stop hitting on her.

Next afternoon Mr. Himmelmann's sister arrived from a distant place to claim the body. The sister was immediately possessed by Beatrice.

"They're laying off at the box factory," Clint told Constance when she took him to his favorite cafeteria after the funeral. Or rather, he took her, since he had a car of sorts. She paid for their meal. He was dressed in a dark suit from some bygone era. Constance guessed he had worn it maybe twice. She couldn't help wondering if people thought she was on a date with him.

"Maybe you'll get lucky," Constance said.

"They're closing the box factory," Clint told her two weeks later, their fourth meal together since the funeral. His calls came several times a day until she finally unplugged the phone. So now if Peter Dodge tried to call her she would never know. Well, he had seemed so crucial to her such a short time ago, but now she was able to examine her own behavior dispassionately. What had made him seem so urgently attractive?

But Clint always found her. And Constance was finding it difficult to be pleasant to him.

"I'm sorry," she repeated with increasing mechanicalness.

"He was so happy that day," Clint would say, his voice more gravelly with each retelling. "He was happy Ulysses had got well. He was happy about his wood critters, you know,

THE EXTINCTION OF RHINOS IN MEXICO

and he had gotten a stall at the swap meet, you know, the one at the drive-in, the one where I showed *Ben Hur* way back when. Happy. And you helped him with the eyes, you were with him when . . ."

Constance mentally began the countdown: *eight seconds, seven, six, we have ignition,* now he would blubber until snot started seeping out that honker of his and then he would want to smother her in a hug.

"And the way you tried to help him . . ." Here came the waterworks *you bitch how dare you youre no daughter of dont touch me again sonuvabitch bastard im sorry i ever fathered you you horrid little well im sorry too you mean heartless spiteful let go of me daddy im leaving good riddance just so you know im getting it done its illegal stupid not in california my god doug shes just a child please daddy i made a mistake its immoral its murder what about me get out of my house get out of my house get out of my house you are dead to me daddy please mama cant you i am sorry dear dont talk to her youre dead to your mother too and your brothers and this whole family we will never speak your name again fuck you i have deaf ears to your foul mouth go to hell daddy you are dead you disgrace you loser you vicious cunt you you you YOU YOU YOU YOU YOU YOU* you sat on the floor gazing up at Kuan Yin, who had always for you understanding, kindness, forgiveness, grace. A smile. A magnificent smile of wood.

* * *

The downstairs of Ernst Himmelmann's house smelled of stale years worth of tv dinners and fried meat, and Constance envisioned the walls gummy with accretions. No one had seen hide nor hair of Ulysses since his tripodal gallop out of the house when the EMS had arrived. The sister busied herself rummaging through Mr. Himmelmann's mail, all business, while Beatrice snooped, all personal. Constance was not sure why she was there herself.

Mr. Himmelmann's sister sighed, appalled at the wild turquoise diningroom.

"What a horrid color scheme."

"Oh I don't know," said Constance.

"You're looking at the lingering evidence of Ernie's last attempt to date, back in '67," Beatrice said.

"He was so shy," said the sister.

"Her name was Ellen DeBerg."

"Yes," said the sister, pointing at Beatrice as her memory was jogged. "That's right, I'd forgotten. Ernie brought her to Sunday supper that year. I can't believe you pulled that woman's name out of the hat."

"Isn't much that escapes Beatrice," Constance said, and Beatrice took it as a compliment.

"She fancied him, but I didn't care for her at all and told her so," said the sister. "She talked Ernie into painting these rooms like this. Ghastly. I gave her a piece of my mind."

"He wasn't a very good judge of people," said Beatrice. She chuckled warmly at the memory.

"Why he didn't repaint after she called it off, I can't imagine," said the sister. "I told him to, I told him. But he was a stubborn coot."

"These were the colors of his love," Constance realized out loud. The sister stared at Constance.

"He was a sweet man, bless him," the sister said.

"What are you going to do about Ulysses?" asked Beatrice.

"Ulysses?"

"His crippled cat," said Beatrice. "Poor thing."

Constance hadn't thought about that.

"Oh, yes. I hate to just abandon the animal. But no telling where he's limped off to."

"Probably lying beside the road somewhere, anyway. Hit

THE EXTINCTION OF RHINOS IN MEXICO

by a car. I mean, just think of him trying to hobble around on those three pathetic legs."

"Oh dear."

"If he shows up, I'll take care of him," Beatrice said.

* * *

Constance awoke in blackness, already forgetting some fading terror, knowing she had heard something. She became alert and present. She heard nothing now, but reached for the M-1. It was 3:17 a.m.

Keeping the darkness, Constance searched each room of her apartment, and, finding nothing, grabbed her flashlight, eased her door open and crept down the carpeted staircase with her rifle, agonizing when a stair creaked. The small white hexagonal tiles of the vestibule were icy on her bare feet.

She heard Ulysses, then, arrooing from inside Mr. Himmelmann's apartment.

She tried the door, but it was locked. She had once seen Mr. H hide a key under the vase on the halfmoon table here, so she picked up the vase. No key. Ulysses called again, mournfully. Inside a bluish green light pulsed.

Out on the icy porch she checked the windows and found the one Mr. H had modified for Ulysses unlocked. She swept the room with her beam . . . the cat eyes reflected and Ulysses blinked. The pulsing blue light was the VCR flashing 12:00 midnight midnight midnight . . .

A tight fit, but she could just make it, squirming through the trapdoor hands down to the floor first and then quickly pulling her rifle through. There was snow stuck between her toes.

Ulysses sat waiting for her, but he would have to wait. She went room by room, slipping in and out like she had learned at Ft. Leonard Wood and later drilled at Incirlik, checking for unfriendlies where the remnants of Mr. Himmelmann's life were already partially gathered and boxed and sealed, while furniture lay beneath shrouds like misshapen corpses.

A thump and clatter in the other room.

Crouching and peering around the corner, Constance saw it was only Ulysses. He arrooed, an apology for having rubbed against one of the Jesus boxes and knocking it over, spilling videotapes onto the floor. This was the last section of the house where Mr. Himmelmann's stuff had yet to be picked through, sorted and denigrated by Beatrice and the sister.

Constance clicked the safety on and set aside the M-1 and flashlight and lifted Ulysses in her arms. He protested, but she hugged him, scratching his graying, whiskered jowls and he thought that wasn't so bad.

"Where you been, boy? Better not let Beatrice catch your ass."

She fixed her flashlight on the floor shining toward the videotapes she started gathering. A label in the beam caught her eye: *Hard Knights*. She collected tapes and put them back in Come Meet My Jesus. *The Adventures of Rod Hershey. Cock Tales. Studs Poker.* Each of the other Jesus boxes had videos all with similar cleverly perverted titles. Constance couldn't help but smile.

Picking one of the videos, she went over to the flashing VCR and pushed the power button. Its wheels and pulleys whirred and she saw there was already a tape in it. The last thing Mr. H had watched. She set down the tape she was holding. One was as bad as another, she figured.

She pulled the OnOff knob to the old console tv and rotated the volume all the way down. A twenty seven inch vision of bright electron snow spread open. She pushed Play and in the silence a smileless youth ambled across the screen, tight belly muscles rippling as he hopped up, sitting naked on a bright kitchen counter, fondling his cock hard. He sprawled his legs. A smiling blonde adonis entered stage left and slid

THE EXTINCTION OF RHINOS IN MEXICO

his erect slick penis into the anus of the youth and thrusted and thrusted and thrusted and thrusted and thrusted—

Constance caught her breath, dizzy like when on the bus at a stoplight there would be another bus next to her, and it would start to move or was her bus moving? Her whole world felt offbalanced, out of kilter. She sat crosslegged in the dark gazing at the naked young men Mr. Himmelmann (and Clint?) had gazed at. *Did you two old men make love, touch tenderly to dispel a fraction of your loneliness?* The flickering, glowing images from the screen danced across her face, and she was curious that she felt herself getting damp, since the images had nothing to do with her, somehow they had all become Lanes and Marcos and Dennises and Peter Dodges; they had found each other, they had no need of her . . .

Is love real or a fluke of chemicals and hormones? Eternal verity or Madison Avenue sizzle? If it feels real, isn't that all that matters? Sometimes feelings are a matter of what you just ate. Who said that? Oh. Scrooge, wasn't it? Well, he was right, the senses are easily fooled. Constance had no emotions left about anything.

She stopped the tape and ejected it. In the tv snow, Constance saw the gloating face of Beatrice Decker floating before her. Constance clamped her eyes shut, shuddering. When she opened them, she saw only her own distorted reflection.

She shut off the tv.

Going quickly to the kitchen, Constance located a garbage bag, into which she emptied the contents of the Jesus boxes and then knotted the bag. Then she made a quick trip upstairs to her own apartment.

She lugged the bundle down the alley to the allnight diner, where she tossed her burden into the dumpster. Soon after, a busboy from the diner came out and found the huipil neatly folded on the lid of the dumpster. He had it properly laundered and took it home to his delighted wife, but Mr. Himmelmann's secret he unknowingly buried, made it safe beneath lettuce cores, sliced tomato ends and limp unserved french fries.

Up in her studio, Constance wept.

In the nightworld the roundfaced wicked witch had a fine, large, weedless crop of suitors dressed in tuxedos standing in a field. Vines grew up tendrils like steel cable snaking through and entwining the legs of these men. The witch began smashing these men over with her garden gloved fists and their heads burst like dandelions, though the tuxedo corpses would spring back upright like the Punching Bozo Constance got for a present when she turned four. From suitor to suitor the hag went knocking each one down until he didn't rise up anymore and one by one they were all dying.

Then Constance found that she was one of these suitors, complete with tuxedo.

The witch smashed and smashed and smashed, closer and closer. Suddenly the witch noticed Constance and came directly for her.

Constance was terrified, but though she thrashed and waved her arms, her feet were rooted by the steel vines.

The crone's arm hauled back, but before she could let loose a haymaker, Constance brilliantly burst all on her own, atomized. *Was it like this for you, Mr. H? The relief of becoming a million dazzling sun sparkles? It's another desire, isn't it? No hurry needed. All the time in the world.* As she glittered, tingled and expanded she could still see the confounded witch far below, surrounded by headless suitors who were somehow all arrooing, but Constance herself was escaping, floating away into joyous dissolution.

* * *

Submerged cerulean and cobalt blues stroked life through ivory blackness with brushed hints at the hidden raging purples within, and deep swaths of alizarin crimson remained, after

THE EXTINCTION OF RHINOS IN MEXICO

all, flickers of titanium white and yellow stretching into tensile ligaments and raw sinews. The image had coalesced, strong and definite.

To the clear, melancholy beauty of Klaus Nomi's woman voice singing the aria from *Samson and Delilah*, Constance completed the stalactites of muscle and the webs of gristle that twisted inside layers inside someplace dark inside her cavernous bardo.

Outside, Beatrice was on her hands and knees strangling an unseasonable weed as she watched hired workmen carting off the last artifacts of Mr. Himmelmann's life. His plywood menagerie had already taken wing, leaving behind only cup hooks.

The basement had been emptied, the old man's legacy of schlock celluloid and tools sold or dispersed to relatives who never laid eyes on him or cared one jot that his father had been an Old World guild gunsmith. Inside his home, where Mr. Himmelmann had lived quietly for so many decades, hired strangers coated paint over his turquoise diningroom and salmon kitchen, suffocating beneath rollers of beige his sole evidence and reminder of a woman's love.

Later that day Constance met Clint at the museum and introduced him to Max, the head security guard, who was looking to fill a vacancy cheaply. She left Mr. Himmelmann's best buddy filling out an application with hope. She herself gave notice at the museum bookstore. She was a responsible sort, her parents had taught her that, and she took pride in it.

As she came up Mr. Himmelmann's sidewalk that afternoon, she saw Ulysses waiting for her on the porch, blinking his cat eyes. She picked him up.

"You're fat, Mr. Arroo. You and I are going on a diet, Mister."

She cradled him up the stairs and set him down while she manicured a bit of pot with the hand painted card of a Mayan shaman beckoning her. This card she kept. She rolled a joint and smoked it, a missed seed popping. While Ulysses galumped around, exploring dust bunnies and twitching his pink nose at odors of the past there in the Hard Cat Shoes studio, Constance sat on her creaking draftsman's swivel stool, one leg tucked up with her arm resting carelessly on the knee as she gazed with an experienced eye, with satisfaction finally, at her finished painting, last of this series. *Time for a Clearance Sale. People always buy your art when they find out you're leaving.*

Constance rocked very slightly on the stool which had very nearly been the platform of her demise and it creaked softly. Its metal frame had an honest patina of age earned during all her father's long hours poring over geologic survey charts. The upholstery was comfortable, a wellworn padded hunter green leather on the seat and backrest. It and a work table had been the only pieces of furniture in his shed office in Cut and Shoot, Texas, "Cut'n'Shoot," where the air smelled of creosote and pine and it seemed like half the young men in town were prison guards over at Huntsville. Daddy used to take her with him out to the various burgs while he paid visits to ranchers and widows whose land lay adjacent to oil strikes by Texaco and Conoco. *And this is my little wildcatter,* presenting his daughter to each of his prospective partners. In a box in her closet she still kept, still hung onto, the photo of her proud Daddy and her younger self, a delighted tomboy hanging off the pipes of an oil well christmas tree like it was her private jungle gym.

Ulysses carefully galumped back over to Constance, staring up at her, at last uttering a patient "Arroo?" His fur was growing over the scar and would eventually cover it completely. She got down on the floor and hugged him to her until he began purring like a motor. The cat watched as Constance spread the map of the world out on the scuffed wooden floor.

Then he lay right on the middle of it.

5

Orion's Belt

After the football game he picked up his son at the junior high locker room. Usually he and his wife served supper at Loaves and Fishes Saturday afternoons, but that morning Mr. MacIntyre had helped cook instead of serve so they could get out of the city early and make the drive well before dark.

A couple of hours later they passed the Cuero water tower and the dip in the road where you crossed the railroad tracks and they drove up into town. The boy saw that the old café on the main street where they had eaten breakfast on their first visit the year before was gone. Torn down. He remembered the ranchers and farmers eating their eggs and toast and sipping their coffee from thick white crockery mugs. Out of politeness a few men had removed and set their hats on the table or the counter, but most of them wore their John Deere gimme caps or sweat stained straw Resistols while they ate. You could see the sungouged creases crisscrossing their burnt necks. They ate and drank quietly, talking some, but softly, like they knew it was going to be another long, hard day, with nothing left for it but to go on and get at it.

The place where the café had been was like a missing tooth. Nothing had been built in its place. Maybe never would be. Down the road there was a new Whataburger with a drivethru.

Now they drove on past the courthouse and the church that looked like an old Spanish mission and got out to the county hospital just as the doctor was walking out to his old pickup. The boy's daddy parked the Volvo in front of the truck and got out. The doctor, who was the chief doctor at the hospital, waved at the lawyer and met him at the curb. Adjusting the rearview mirror, the boy watched the two men talking behind him.

Ever since the boy could remember, his mom and daddy had been telling stories about the doctor. That is, when they talked about their youth, which was not often. The boy's daddy scorned nostalgia. He preferred "the here and now," he called it, or else planning the future. And the boy liked that. He supposed his daddy's stance had something to do with being an attorney, although the boy also knew that at least part of the law depended on the past.

The doctor dressed like a ranch hand and seemed like somebody from the movies. Like James Dean grown older and taller. But it was the scar that had captured the boy. It started almost at the doctor's left ear and ran along down to the doctor's mouth, pinching it at the edge, making his smile a lopsided, rakish thing. The boy could scarcely believe the tall man had been his daddy's best friend since back when they were still boys. When the doctor moved down here to Texas, it had been years since either man laid eyes on the other.

The attorney agreed to let his son ride out to the ranch with the doctor in the old Dodge pickup the doctor had owned since high school. When they climbed in the truck, the doctor looked the boy over.

"Good Lord, but you're a big sonuvagun. How come you let that Mexican run over you on the kickoff?"

Huge runner barreling down on him. Open field. The boy froze like a deer caught in headlights. Then the brick wall with legs slammed into him, leveled him, never slowed down for him. The boy choked back dusty tears inside his helmet.

"I should've kept my feet moving and driven through

THE EXTINCTION OF RHINOS IN MEXICO

him with my legs."

"That's the way your daddy used to do 'em."

The doctor started the truck toward the ranch, with the daddy following.

"You did nail that one poor bastard, though."

Fourth down, goalline stand. A faked kick, then a pitch—a sweep to his side. The boy penetrated the line, drove his shoulder hard into the halfback five yards deep. Knocked the stocky runner on his back. Prevented the score. Twisted his ankle, but he scarcely noticed it in the heat of the moment.

The boy tried to think of words which caught how that play had felt. Great. Perfect. Primo. Primal? No words did it.

"Thanks."

"Too bad y'all couldn't score again."

"That's what Coach said. Yelled, actually."

"Damn right he yelled. Christ, a tie's like kissin' your sister. How's the ankle?"

"Hurts."

The boy liked riding through the autumn countryside beneath the muscular gray overcast, down the two lane farm-to-market road in the faded green truck. He liked the broad fenders you could sit on like John Wayne in *Hatari*, and the short running board back under the spare tire on the side. A shotgun lay across the rack along the back window of the cab. Through that window the boy could see his daddy following them in the Volvo. His daddy waved.

"Can you whip your father yet?"

"No sir."

"Hell, he'll probably be kickin' our asses when he's eighty."

When he was little, the boy had delighted in ordering his daddy to "make a bowling ball." His daddy would laugh and curl his arm. The man's biceps were smooth convex steel, like Popeye's, and you could practically hear the muscles clink if you rapped on them. His daddy was older and heavier now, but on him the weight was rock that simply gave him more mass to dominate you with. At home in the backyard during their sessions on proper tackling and blocking form, his daddy would demonstrate on the boy, and in the mock tackles that sometimes took his breath away he could feel his father's reined-in power. Whenever their arguments heated up, the boy would recall that might. The boy did not like the arguing. It happened more these days, and afterwards the compulsion of it would always scare him, but sometimes he had to say what he thought, tell his daddy what he felt about things.

"Bet you didn't know your daddy did his share of hellraisin' when he was in high school," the doctor said.

"No lie?"

"Christ, he was an instigator," said the doctor. "Don't let that rational lawyer demeanor fool you."

He steered onehanded while reaching under the seat. He pulled out a bottle of clear liquid.

"How tall are you now?" the doctor asked. "What do you weigh?"

"Six two, a hundred and sixty five pounds."

"Jesus, the moment you were born I saw you'd grow up to be a bruiser."

He bit the plastic topped cork out and handed the bottle to Brad.

"Take a whiff of that."

It made Brad's eyes water and his nostrils burn. He handed the bottle back.

"What the heck is it?"

"White lightnin'. Arkansas moonshine. Some friends back in Gurdon distill it themselves."

The doctor tossed his head back, upending the bottle, and his adam's apple bobbed. Then he wiped his mouth and checked in the rearview mirror.

"Now don't you be sneakin' any sips of this. Jack'd skin

me alive." The scar stretched with his lopsided grin.

Once when he only reached his daddy's waist, the boy's mom had let him sip beer from her glass. It had tasted fizzy and metallic. He had wanted to spit it out, and the adults had all been amused by the face they said he made. The boy hated the taste of alcohol unless it was in something very sweet. And then he had to drink it fast. Right before the Halloween dance this year he had drunk a whole bottle of Strawberry Hill. But he preferred smoking pot. It was friendlier.

"You should've seen it. There I am, drivin' like a maniac, your papa's standin' in the bed of this truck shootin' a beebee gun back at a gang of hoodlums in hotrods who're chasin' us through the woods outside of town."

"How come they were after you?"

"To tell the truth, son, I forget. But it probably had somethin' to do with defendin' Ginny's honor."

The boy tried to picture it.

"You said from the moment I was born."

"That's right."

"You were there?"

"Damned if I was gonna stand for Ginny goin' it alone."

"What about Daddy?"

"Well, your padre had law school finals down in Dallas. Couldn't miss those. Too much at stake."

"Could I try that?"

The doctor looked over at the boy. Skin grafts had gentled the screaming red, but had not hidden its menace altogether. He grinned his scar smile.

"Well I don't calculate a swig would send you straight to hell."

The boy drank a mouthful, paused, then swallowed. He shuddered. His tongue burned and he felt he'd been kicked in the stomach. He handed the bottle back to the doctor.

"Man," the boy said.

The doctor took another long drink.

"Yeah, your mother and I and Jack had our share of adventures."

After a while they came to the place before the train tracks where you drove down off the road onto the dirt ruts through the grass to the gate of the ranch. The doctor got out and unlocked and opened the wide swinging gate made of welded pipe. He waved at the boy to come on through.

The boy sat there. He had a student license, but a standard shift was still only theory. He could feel his father waiting, looking at him back there, and that made his face hot. Or maybe it was the moonshine. His ankle was throbbing, but it hardly hurt now.

He scooted over into the driver's seat and studied the column shift lever. All the angry driving sessions came back to him and he could hear his father losing patience with his son's whiplashing attempts to shift. *Don't clutch up.* His father's driving joke, and it made the boy smile now. He found first gear and eased out on the pedal. The truck lurched, then the gear engaged smoothly forward. The boy's daddy drove in behind him. When truck and car were through, the doctor walked the gate shut and refastened the chain.

The doctor drove the truck swaying slowly over the uneven ruts and cowpaddies. A clump of dark cattle left their huddle beneath the gnarly, majestic oak that shielded them against the north wind. Here they came, plodding, then trotting after the vehicles. In real life, cattle were big.

"Dumb brutes."

"Yeah, they look pretty dense," said the boy.

"Aw, they think every time they see you you're bringin' food for them," said the doctor. "Kind of like welfare bums." He chuckled. The boy laughed, too, then regretted it. He had laughed without thinking, to be friends with the doctor.

"You ever go hunting with Daddy?" the boy asked.

"Rabbits occasionally, but he never was that excited about

THE EXTINCTION OF RHINOS IN MEXICO

the sport. Your daddy's killin' instinct has been funneled into the courtroom."

Joslin was standing on the wood porch waiting for them as they drove up. Joslin was the caretaker of the ranch. He was very fat and his face was pigmented by sun and booze. As they pulled up, he spewed a burst of tobacco juice out on the ground.

A stereotype, the boy thought. Maybe the archetype, he smiled. He had read "archetype" in a book recently, and his daddy had made him look it up in the dictionary. The boy liked how as soon as you learned a word, it came in handy.

The boy's daddy got out of the family car and came over.

"How's your ankle feeling?" he asked the boy.

"Still sore when I walk on it."

"Come on in and we'll pack it in ice for a while," the doctor ordered. "Joslin, we got ourselves two generations of football hero here. Father and son."

"Good deal."

"Brother's on first string offense and defense. Played a pretty fair ballgame today."

"You were there?" asked the boy's daddy.

"Be a real hoss once he grows into his frame," Joslin spat.

"Jack here had a college football scholarship. Could've turned pro."

"No kiddin'."

"No, he is kidding," the boy's father said, and then laughed.

"One of the finest prospects ol' Smoo had at the time."

"Oh, Dell, I was not."

"The hell you weren't."

"They were thinking of cutting me from the team."

But the boy could hear the pride in his daddy's voice.

"Problem was," the doctor explained, "he got his knee busted up before he proved he could lick his one weakness as a player."

"Dell, you've got a penchant for the melodramatic."

"Now, Jack, denial is always going to prevent a recovery."

"Drop it. It's ancient history."

"Have you taught Brother here any history? Sure hate to see him repeat it."

The boy looked at the doctor. The shift had been sudden.

"'Brad' is his name," said the boy's daddy. "Not 'Brother' or 'Junior.'"

The boy recognized the smiling his daddy used to temper irritation.

"All right, Jack. Don't get bent all out of shape."

"Well."

"All I'm gettin' at is that I'm tickled to death to see Brad here rarin' to emulate you. Hell, the torch has been passed."

"Actually I don't know that I want to play after this year," the boy said.

The men all looked at him.

"Why that's the most ridiculous thing I ever heard," said the doctor with a half grin. "When did he decide this, Jack?" Disappointment seemed to spill from the doctor's lopsided smile.

"I've just been thinking about it," the boy said.

"What on God's earth for?"

"Dell, it's his decision to make."

"I just hate to see you let him throw away his Godgiven talent."

"I've got other talents, I think."

"Son, that's not the point."

"Dell, it's none of your business." Brad knew that flat tone. It left no room for discussion. Joslin shifted his chaw to the other cheek. The doctor grinned.

"Look, just tell me to shut up," he said. "Brad, we'll get your ankle in shape for next week's game, anyway."

"You probably shouldn't be standing on that much right

THE EXTINCTION OF RHINOS IN MEXICO

now," said the boy's father.

"I'm ok."

"You may feel fine right this minute, but a few hours walking around in the cold and you'll be changing your tune."

"He's right, Brother."

"We'll set you up in a blind," said Joslin. He spat brown.

The house inside was a house kept by men. An ancient radio was barely hanging onto a scratchy country western station.

"Welcome to the Nekkid Lady Room," said the doctor. Slickpaged color magazine photos overspread the wooden wall of the main room, years of lounging Miss Octobers and Miss Julys overlapped by more recent, less genteel spreads and garish closeups. The boy tried not to stare. He wanted to go study each one separately. This way it was a staggering saturation of raw Woman.

The doctor poured himself a drink and held up the bottle for the daddy and Joslin. Joslin drooled and spat into an old beer bottle, and joined the doctor.

"I'll pass," said the boy's daddy. On the radio "Blue Eyes Crying In the Rain" filtered through the static.

"Listen to that," said the doctor. He closed his eyes. "That man has got to be the best singer in the world. Bar none."

"Jennifer and I have a couple of Willie's records," said Mr. MacIntyre.

"He's pretty good," the boy offered.

"The man's magnificent. Nobody can touch him."

Joslin nodded reverently.

"Don't get carried away," the boy's daddy said.

"Jack, he may just be the greatest singer of all time."

"You're already drunk," the boy heard his daddy say. He could tell his daddy was trying to kid his old friend, but was a little rusty at it.

"I am an alcoholic," said the doctor. "Of course I have

been drinking, but I am not close to drunk. And the truth would be the same even if I was sober."

In the bedroom it smelled musty and vaguely like a locker room. On the chipped veneer of a once elegant chest of drawers, dusty black and white photographs stood in jumbled frames like headstones in a neglected cemetery.

There was one at a lake showing the doctor, the boy's mother and his daddy. His mother's swimming suit was a dated onepiece. Everybody was lean and smiley. His mother looked surprisingly cute standing between the youths, her arm around each of them. Because the picture had faded, the boy could not be certain, but it looked like the doctor did not have the scar on his face. He sure looked like James Dean.

One of the other pictures was a wedding picture of the doctor. The bride was gorgeous. He had heard his parents talking about the doctor's several wives. The boy picked up a tarnished frame that held the doctor and the boy's mother at a formal dance. They looked cool as hell together.

After they stowed their gear, the boy's daddy insisted that the doctor sober up some before they did any shooting. They looked around the ranch, and later the doctor brought out the rifles and let the boy and his daddy take practice shots at some beer cans on a fence rail. The heavy realness and kick of the rifle scared the boy, but he shot okay with it. He watched his daddy shoot and was impressed what a good shot he was, how familiar he seemed to be with the weapon and its handling.

"Now we'll see how you do when there's eyes at the other end of the barrel," the doctor said. He blew into his hands to warm them; the light had grayed and it was getting colder.

THE EXTINCTION OF RHINOS IN MEXICO

* * *

The boy had been sitting for a long time in the limbo of the autumn overcast, cramped and crouched in the deer blind hammered together out of plywood and painted camouflage. Crumpled Jax and Schlitz cans lay with sunfaded Cheetos and Slim Jim wrappers littering the ground around the blind, and the floor inside it also documented several seasons of hunting. He listened, but did not hear the other men nor any shots. The clearing was empty but for three mesquite trees that had been left standing. Corn had been grown in the field so the deer would get used to eating there.

He felt thick in his winter layers, but the north wind still nipped his nose. He would have sworn the plank he was sitting on was harder than any wood in the summer, and the cold soaked right up through to his bottom.

A shot cracked far off in the woods to his left.

Who was it?

The light was failing, the mesquites smudging into a shadowy mass. The boy's ankle was really throbbing now and his toes had gone numb. He would be glad when it got dark and he could go back into the warm house.

The boy wished he had kept his mouth shut about football. He felt bad about disappointing his daddy. He wondered what the weakness was that the doctor had been jabbing his daddy about.

Glancing out then, he saw the deer.

One, two-three-four, five—no, six—at least ten of them, grazing far across the clearing. He must have been daydreaming to not have seen them drift into the open.

For some time he did not move, certain he would spook the deer. Then he remembered to breathe and felt the rifle: dense, cleanlined metal and wood, cold even through the gloves. Carefully he used his teeth to remove the glove from his triggerfinger hand. The glove dropped and the boy froze again.

The deer grazed serenely.

His hand felt small and distinct and dexterous after the thickness of the glove. Slowly he raised the rifle, conscious of its precisefeeling weight, and slid the barrel out the opening in the blind. Looking through the scope pleased him the way it made the deer closer and easier to see.

Through the scope he spotted three very young deer, five doe and two he was not sure of. He scanned the field again. Yes, there were two bucks, he could see the antlers.

OK, pick one.

The crosshairs bobbed, then settled pretty well on the buck. Not good enough. He wanted to be certain, and he could not seem to hold still. Then he remembered to shift the safety off. He settled and re-aimed. Head down, nibbling the grass, the deer took two steps that put a branch between him and death.

The boy cussed to himself. He swallowed, rolled his shoulders to loosen up, then sighted through the scope again. The second buck was head on but moving. Now he was turning to present a perfect shot. The crosshairs met at the deer's right shoulder.

But it was so far away. Could he hit it from here? It was already pretty dark. What if he botched it and only crippled it or something? Was it too dark already? He aimed once more. Maybe they would still move closer. How far was it?

The boy sat poised for an unknown time, frozen in the silence between instants.

The rifle kicked him hard in the shoulder, the bullet jumped the distance to the deer and it was like the boy shot out with the bullet and hit the deer himself with a smack impact he felt a blink before the monstrous riflefiring crack shoved out against the blind and bounced back to envelop his head.

THE EXTINCTION OF RHINOS IN MEXICO

All the deer bolted with beautiful boundings and leapings, vanishing gracefully into the brush. His ears rang. How could he have missed? Certain he had not missed, he ran out, covering ground quickly to the spot where the deer had stood moments before.

He looked all around, and then suddenly, even in the twilight, his huntstimulated vision detected the speckles of blood on the grass. He rejoiced, feeling he could lift a house.

In a rush he feared he might still lose the deer in the thicket, in the coming darkness, and never find it. He crouched along the ground, locating viscous drops that would have been crimson in daylight, but which at this late hour appeared black.

Dry grasses grew kneehigh along the perimeter of the clearing. Through this he tracked it, wary of the cactus and heading toward the darkening tangle of thorny huisache and mesquite. His heart drummed.

He almost stumbled over the buck. It lay at his feet a scant ten yards from the edge of the clearing. It lay breathtakingly full and large and, in the gloaming, dun colored on a bed of long tawny grass, like a bright offering.

Maybe it wasn't dead. It might thrash about horrifically and struggle as he tried to put it out of its misery.

But the animal was dead all right. Through his being flashed an exhilaration of balance, a sensation like the very first time he realized his father had let go of the bicycle without telling him. He slowly kneeled and placed his bare hand on its weight and pelt and the startling soft firmness of the neighbor girl's breast when they first kissed in her backyard breached his awareness and was gone. The large deer body still held a warm denseness of life, the dynamic muscles now stilled, yet still pliant. Life hovered around the so recently alive creature, and the boy felt some of its energy come into him. He breathed, aware of his breathing. Never had he looked on anything so completely satisfying as the simple intricacies of browns and whites in the bristles of its fur, and the sadness over him possessed a different quality than the remorse he had expected.

The boy heard something and turned. The doctor appeared, tromping the grasses.

"You got one, Brother," he grinned like a rogue. He stuck a Lucky Strike between his lips and lighted it. Then he got the boy to help him drag the kill out into the clearing.

They stood up to catch their breath. The doctor pulled a small silver flask from a zippered pocket in his coveralls. He guzzled a swig, then offered it to the boy. The boy took a quick mouthful and handed the flask back to the doctor. The boy swallowed and squinched his eyes. The alcohol taste made him dizzy and nauseated, but this time the spreading heat in his innards became elation.

They waited for the other men to show up. While they waited, the doctor paced off the distance. Then the daddy walked over with Joslin.

"Good hundred and twenty yards," said the doctor.

So far, thought the boy. It seemed unfair somehow. Yet he felt the swell of pride at his acknowledged marksmanship.

"Spike," said Joslin with a heavy grunt.

"Biggest goddamn buck I ever saw that was only a spike," the doctor said. "I've seen 'em smaller than this with six points."

"Could be somethin' about the food supply this season."

"I missed," said the boy's daddy.

"You never had much of a shot in the first place, Jack," said the doctor.

"The youngster here showed us all up," Joslin said.

"I thought I missed at first," said the boy. "But I heard it hit and came over and found the blood on the grass."

"Lookie here how small that entrance wound is," the doctor said. He poked at the red hole that was smaller than his finger. "Give me a hand, here, Brother."

The boy helped the doctor roll the deer over. The weight

THE EXTINCTION OF RHINOS IN MEXICO

of it surprised him. The animal seemed to have gotten heavier. The hole on the other side was scarcely the size of a nickel.

"Might have gotten it in the lungs."

The boy's father knelt and touched the deer experimentally himself, looking it over. The boy stood over his father watching. Suddenly the boy felt bad about the deer. His daddy had never got a deer, and though that did not matter to the man, now his kid had killed one and he was the only one there who never had.

"Good shot," the father said.

"Thanks."

"Natural born shot," said the doctor. "You hearin' footsteps, Jack?"

"No."

"Why should he hear footsteps?" asked Joslin.

"There I go talkin' football again," said the doctor.

"I'd forgotten how funny you can be," the lawyer said.

The boy felt them spoiling it.

"I aimed at it for a long time and couldn't pull the trigger."

"Buck fever," said Joslin with a phlegmy chuckle.

"You beat it, though, that's the important part," said the doctor. He looked at Brad's daddy. "I've seen grown men freeze up and let a herd of deer walk by. You never know 'til you're in that position."

"Have to whip you up some eggs and deer brains in the mornin'," said Joslin.

"What?"

"Scrambled eggs and deer brains. Time honored tradition to celebrate your first kill."

"You don't have to eat it if you don't want to, Brad."

"I don't mind, Daddy. As long as they're not just kidding me."

"Hell no I'm not kidding. It's a perquisite," said the doctor.

"Oh, Dell, that's ridiculous."

"Better than pussy," said Joslin.

The boy sat down on the ground abruptly.

"Man, my ankle's killing me," the boy said, just realizing the fact. "I ran all the way over here looking for the deer and didn't even think about it."

"I daresay you had a healthy jolt of adrenaline coursing through your veins," said the doctor.

"Yeah, I felt strong."

"Kid's got a hunter's instinct alright," said Joslin.

Joslin brought out a lantern. He lit it and held it up, and by its hissing glare the doctor cut out the guts while the boy's father assisted, and then they sliced away the damp, heavy furskin. Now it was simply a carcass and there was no feeling to be had about it anymore. They were men the boy was glad to be with right then, even Joslin. As they field dressed the meat, the boy liked sitting there on the camp stool, watching his daddy's face and still muscular body in the lantern glow, and the doctor's clean, surehanded bladework. He liked that Dell and Daddy had been friends for so long and that they been rivals for his mother's hand.

A dry norther was gusting sharply by the time they hauled the meat to hang in a cold shed overnight and tossed the guts out into the dark clearing for the coyotes.

The wind cleared the sky and plunged the mercury below freezing. That night they ate panfried venison with slices of white bread and peeled, boiled potatoes. The men all got drunk in the woodstove heat of the drafty Nekkid Lady Room. The youngest man found that Schlitz didn't taste that bad after the first few and the buzz made him friendly and loud enough to keep up with the doctor. He would liked to have gone out and smoked some weed, but he did not like being high around adults.

Towards one a.m. the doctor got even louder and instigated the arm wrestling contests, not taking No for an answer. Brad barely beat Joslin, then struggled and defeated the doctor. He had wanted to best the doctor.

THE EXTINCTION OF RHINOS IN MEXICO

Before taking on his dad, he went outside. The brittle air came sharp and cleanly cold into his lungs and cleared his head some. As he pissed out a little ways from the old house, he gazed up at the black vault of the country night sky. Out of the haze of stars he could pick only a few constellations, but Orion the Hunter was one he was sure of. The young man recalled being six and his father pointing out the three bright stars of the belt to him. It still awed him that the diamond blue light he was seeing now had started twinkling toward earth centuries ago. All that time and distance from an instant, and the instant endured. The thought always made him feel settled. The young man suddenly remembered again the killing and it was there even now, alive and clear and solid, at the core of his drunkenness, and he understood it was different than the doctor's killing. In his swirling head he knew his mother had made the best choice and the boy wished his daddy had gotten the deer instead. He did not want to beat his dad tonight. He wanted to never beat him.

6

THE SMELL OF A CHRISTIAN

Lumberjack was in back chopping off fish heads, Baron was outside threatening to piss on the air conditioner again, and there still weren't no sign of Big Max when they started to hit us hard. Bert, if you never cooked the Line one man short on a fourth of July Saturday night, then you ain't never experienced heat. It was nothing to me, though, and I'd been up for six days straight. I was shooting for a personal record of seven whole days, a solid week of altered consciousness, and couldn't stop jamming now for more than two minutes in a row without my hands shaking like a dog shitting peach pits.

The fryers were boiling like mad with overloads of fries, chicken titties and okra, so I went back to the prep table where El Jack was decapitating salmon and laying the filets in a tub of ice.

Lumberjack slapped the wall with a rag.

"I think I just killed Gregor Samsa," he said.

"I'm for wasting all commies," I said. "Switch the music to high octane."

He cleaned his hands and tuned the big dial. Him a Nam vet college boy and there I was, a ninth grade dropout, ordering him around. He reached up to the shelf that held various cook supplies and our radio. Used to all we had was a beat up, flour encrusted little Radio Shack portable with a bent coat hanger antenna. Then one day Big Max had lugged in this antique after he bought his senile mother a new setup. It

THE EXTINCTION OF RHINOS IN MEXICO

was a classic, Bert, an old 1940s wooden cased tubemeister. Big Max was very proud of it.

El Jack rolled the dial til he found somebody jackhammering a guitar.

"Yey-uh!" I hollered and got back to work. A kitchen with no tunes ain't got a pulse. Rupert came back from out front through the east swinging door, which we called Door Number 2, like in *Let's Make a Deal*, remember that show? He had his hands tucked inside his full length apron above the waist tie.

"Say, Iceman, what's the name of that new jailbait doorwhore Tully hired?"

"Lily."

"Well get ready. Lily got a waiting list out there long as my dick."

"Oh goodie, we'll be home early."

Rupert did a quick Michael Jackson spinaround and pointed at me with a scowl.

"In case you didn't know, I'm puttin' a hex on your monkey Mexican ass."

"I don't believe in nothing that ain't scientifically proven."

"Big Max still ain't showed?"

"Do you hear him? Do you see him? Do you smell him?"

"Well, good luck."

He laughed, took off his apron and shot it into the dirty bag like a basketball.

"Hey, Bert, where do you think you're going?" I asked him.

"To my life. I done my time."

"Your shift ain't over til Max shows up."

He twisted his mouth and glared at me, but he tied on a fresh apron.

Then here come Stacy Clarke rushing in through Door Number 1, the south swinging door, and she pushes me a ticket. Stacy had an ego as big as her naturally red hair. Her goal in life was to be as important an actress as Tina Louise.

Stacy was a natural 10 and a half and Bert she used it. But then Tully never did hire ugly waitrons.

"Iceman, please, these people have been sitting there for half an hour."

"And why is that, pray tell?"

She hesitated, but she knew it ain't no good to lie to the Iceman.

"It's so busy I forgot to turn in the ticket."

I wiped my brow with my arm, butcher knife in hand.

"I suppose you want me to rush the order?"

"I'll be your best friend."

I ran my finger along the line of tickets clipped across the window, then down to the overflow stack of more tickets. I picked up Stacy's and put it on the bottom.

She whimpered, picked up the plates of a finished order and fled, vanishing out Door Number 1, passing Steve the bartender, who was ferrying a Shiner Bock on a tray.

"Bar order, amigo," he said. Steve had a beard, but he kept it closely trimmed. He was a sensitive guy: his patron saint was Sam Malone.

"Hand it over, Bert."

Steve gave me the ticket for a fried chicken breast sandwich with fries, then slipped me the longneck so no one else would see it.

"Listen, the sooner you can get that order out..."

"Got you covered, Steverino."

Soon as he left, I stuck his ticket on the bottom of the stack with Stacy's. Steve always thought he had the angle figured. Yet he was working extra shifts, so what does that tell you? He'd just gotten back from Vegas. Every year he was certain he had a system worked out. Every year he'd blow a bundle and have to come back early. I eased my beautiful dark amber beer into a tumbler, eightysixed the bottle, then poked a straw into my refreshing glass of "ginger ale."

THE EXTINCTION OF RHINOS IN MEXICO

"Iceman, I'll do that rush order for her," Rupert said, his back to me as he worked.

"No you won't."

He turned to me. "I'd *like* to have Stacy be my best friend."

"You don't want a friend, you want a playmate. Like Miss July."

He grumbled but went back to tending the grill. Lumberjack went out back and pulled six or seven beef tenderloins out of the smoker and brought them in on a tray. Graceful as a dancer, Rachel Trudeau breezed in onehanding a tray loaded with glasses of ice tea.

"Thought you fellas could use something to cool you down."

Rachel was our head waitress, a lifer, Cajun by birth and temper. Rachel would have been at home in a truckstop, only she had an addiction to fashionable clothes, good wine and beautiful people. Rachel herself was a run of the mill blonde, pretty when she spent a half hour or so on her makeup and another hour in wardrobe.

I hid my glass of beer in the clutter of the Line and took one of her glasses of tea and held it cool to the bandana around my steaming forehead.

"Ice tea for the Iceman. I'd say that's appropriate. Six days straight so far, Rachel. Or I should say, six days altered, six days and counting."

"You just gonna end up sleeping a week when you done," she said.

"Doesn't work that way," said Dix, the old hippie dishwasher, as he and Lumberjack each grabbed a glass. Rupert took his and gulped it.

"I sure do appreciate it, Rachel," he said.

"You welcome, Rupert. You the only gentleman of the bunch." She was aiming her last remark at Lumberjack, knowing it would get him.

"Nice to know somebody round here appreciates me," Rupert said. He was the only guy I ever knew who could strut in place.

Lumberjack stumbled over his tongue to make amends and thank Rachel. She arched her eyebrows at him and smiled, pleased with her effect. All things considered, she was holding up pretty well.

Rupert yanked out three fish filets and laid them sizzling with butter in the big skillet. Rachel fished Stacy's ticket from the bottom of the stack and put it to me.

"How about it, Hobart?"

"That's Captain Hobart to you."

She had known me from the days back in San Antonio when I was fifteen and my dad the Great Santini had booted me out of the house and Tully, an assistant manager fresh out of college, had put me in charge of dishwashing.

"This table's being real assholes. Poor girl's about to bust into tears."

I looked at Rachel, at her insisting eyes, her remembered lips, and picked up the ticket almost against my will.

"We got a Priority One, Rupert."

Rupert checked the ticket and started the food. I turned and Rachel was right there, had come back around the side.

"What?" I said. The way she was looking at me, I stepped out of the hotbox.

"You know last week..." she was talking almost quieter than I could hear, which certainly ain't her style. "I was wondering, I know I was pretty wasted... Did you and me...?"

I waved her away. "Nothin'," I told her. "I fell asleep. No offense."

Rachel's eyes smiled at me. She picked up her orders, made a big noisy kiss in the air at me and exited.

"Don't make me no nevermind if Big Max shows up or not," Rupert said. We were shoulder to shoulder in the cramped space. "That big ugly honkey scares me."

THE EXTINCTION OF RHINOS IN MEXICO

"No lie, Bert." Me and Rupert didn't see eye to eye on a whole menu of issues, but I had to agree with him there. Lumberjack, on the other hand, had the nasty habit of getting along with everybody.

"Come on, you guys," he piped in. "Max is a pussycat. I mean, he lives with his invalid mother."

"Dig it. Just like in *Psycho*," said Rupert. He poked a ribeye, gauged the blood, then flipped it.

"That was just a movie."

"So? Charlie Manson was just a family man too. And he wasn't no Hollywood story."

Lumberjack laughed. "Actually he was."

"Hey," I said. "Who gave the order to chuckle?"

He hadn't been there the night Max came in late, tripping, right at the start of the rush, and told me to open my mouth. I did, naturally, and he popped a tab of acid onto my tongue. Yeah, Bert, that was one weird shift. High pressure cooking is rough enough without your plates melting and crawling across the floor. I had to step out back and dunk my head in a bucket of ice for about a half hour. It was one of the rare times I have been humbled by drugs.

"Wouldn't surprise me one bit if Big Max was boofing," Rupert said.

"How you figure that?" asked El Jack.

"Look how weird he is."

"Doesn't take crack for that."

"He's on probation for armed robbery, I know that much."

"With a water pistol."

"My point exactly!" said Rupert. "He fuck with me, I cut him."

"Yeah, you bad," I said. He turned on me.

"I can do the same for you, Ice. Just keep it up. Coming at you, man."

Rupert lunged across me as he spatulaed burgers and chicken on bun setups for half a dozen plates.

"Medium rare, well, medium cheese, medium Swiss, bacon mushroom and one chicken titty. Heh!"

He twirled his spatula like a gunslinger. He was always saying "Heh!" like he thought he was James Brown.

"That sort of thing tends to run in families," Dix drawled. "Craziness, I mean. Excuse me."

Then it hit us. Everyone groaned and Rupert fanned the air.

"Dix, you make *me* want to run," he said. "How come you always farting and then saying Excuse me?"

"Just being polite."

"Well, Mr. Silent But Deadly, it would be a whole lot politer if you just quit gassing us."

Baron yowled again.

"Ol' Baron smells fish," Lumberjack said.

"It ain't the fish," I said.

"Max never should've fed that ol' tom in the first place," Rupert grumbled.

"You want some cheese with that whine?" I asked.

"And I suppose you *like* the way the air conditioner smells?"

The second wave hit us then and all the waitrons seemed to barge in from both doors at once throwing multiple orders at us.

"Incoming!" I shouted. "Yee hah!" I had Dix crank up the volume on the radio. A gal named Sylvia, very tan, very short, very cute, studying math at the university, slapped down a handful of tickets. She was so petite, she was what I call a spinner.

"Order in!" Sylvia said. "Rupert, did you see the fireworks over the bay?"

"Now how would I do that, honey? They been working my ass. Can't see nothing back here except orders. But if you like, I can show you some fireworks when I get off tonight."

"I'm pretty sure they'll be over by then." She winked.

THE EXTINCTION OF RHINOS IN MEXICO

"Waitrons should be obscene, not heard," I said.

"Amen," Rupert grumbled.

Sylvia collected the plates of her ready orders and dashed out as Rachel came in and deposited her own tickets.

"Order in!" Rachel hollered for each ticket. "Order in! Why them jackasses picking on us? Order in!"

"I hear the IRS is sticking it to waitresses all over the country," said Angie, a pointy faced ex homecoming queen. She was adding an ice tea to her tray.

"I know *I* am," I said.

Rachel and Angie gave me drop dead smiles. All over town the tax man had a lot of waitron and bartender bowels in an uproar. He was going back and checking records. If they hadn't declared some minimum average of tips, the feds were nailing these tax rebels for back taxes and penalties. Yeah, Bert, that was sure to fix the national debt.

"Hard to say if Sam is our uncle or our Big Brother," said Dix to no one in particular.

"What are you bellyaching about?" I said. "Nobody here tips the kitchen anyway." Futile protests from the waitrons. The dumbwaiter rattled down from upstairs. As Rachel struggled to unload the plates, Prince Lumberjack galloped over to the rescue.

"Why, thank you, Brad," she said, flashing him her smile. Rachel may not have been a centerfold, but when she smiled at you that way, it made you certain you were the dude that hung the moon.

"You know, Jefferson invented the dumbwaiter," Lumberjack was saying to her as they loaded the dumbwaiter together.

"Who?"

"Thomas Jefferson. You know, Declaration of Independence?"

"Oh. When you said Jefferson, I thought you meant George."

I saw him start to laugh, then realize she wasn't kidding.

"The reference was a little esoteric," he allowed.

"Sugar, what are you babbling about?"

He gazed at her until she blushed. She pushed the button sending the rattlyass dumbwaiter up and then escaped through Door Number 1.

"Who invented the dumb cook?" I called to Lumberjack as he came on back. Rupert pulled out the empty tenderloin tray.

"Don't be wasting your eyeballs, College Boy," said Rupert. "Boss man leaves 'em, Iceman retrieves 'em."

"That's the natural order around here, Bert," I told Lumberjack. "Now slice me some of that fresh tendergroin."

As Rupert was passing the tenderloin tray I accidentally on purpose bumped it, sloshing blood from the tray onto Lumberjack. You should've seen him jump.

"Don't be afraid, Richie Cunningham," laughed Rupert. He never bought that Lumberjack had actually been to Nam. "It's only a little cow juice."

"Yeah, no use crying over spilt blood," I said. I had doubts myself. He seemed too wimpy, despite his decent build. Too nice. You couldn't get him to tell you nothing about being in country, neither.

Rupert nudged him while he was mopping his white shirt with a rag.

"What's blonde pussy like?"

"I give up."

"Oh, you wouldn't know about that, would you?"

"Maybe I just think you shouldn't talk about it."

"I knew I was right! Heh!" He elbowed me in the ribs. "He's cutting in on you Iceman. I *figured* she'd be on the rebound after Tully gave her walking papers."

Brad shook his head and smiled with one side of his mouth. He could deny it all he wanted, but even if he wasn't getting any, he couldn't help but enjoy the fact that guys thought he was.

"No, man. We like to drink wine. That's it."

"I may be black, but I ain't dumb."

"We're just friends."

"What good is that?"

When I wasn't looking, Vaughn Mead had slipped in through the back door. Appropriate. You don't find them much tall dark and handsomer than Vaughn. But the ladies were wasting their time drooling over that beefcake. He was a San Francisco brother, if you catch my drift, Bert. He was always scheduled to start his shift later than any other waitron on account of his AM radio show running to 6:30 p.m. Hardly mattered if he showed up late anyhow; it was tough to catch Vaughn ever doing any actual work. I figure Tully put up with Vaughn's goldbricking because he was so good at honeydripping the customers.

I had two chicken titties in the fryer, a rare ribeye on the grill and my burners all covered with salmon sautéing, smothered steak and sautéing squash and zucchini. When I got the chance, I turned and saw Vaughn back with El Jack, who now had about fifty dinner salads working.

"You guys hear my show?" He was chatting in his gleeful way, grabbing extra sprouts and olives for a customized salad he was hijacking. El Jack didn't look happy about it, but he was letting Vaughn slide, and that don't cut it in my kitchen.

"No," said Lumberjack. "The, uh, radio's been acting up."

"Too bad. I said some clever things."

Dix, El Cosmic Dishwasher, moseyed in Door Number 2 hauling a bustub of dirty dishes. The waitrons darted around him, leaving orders, picking up orders, flying out again. Dix was a sloth among hummingbirds.

"So what do you think of Tully's new Jag?" Vaughn asked El Jack.

"It's his pride and joy," Lumberjack said, and I thought I

detected some admirable sarcasm.

"Actually, it's a used Jaguar, red, model XKE," said Professor Dix. "Itself somewhat a collector's item, only he took out the twelve cylinder and had an American V-8 put in. If you ask me, what's the point, then?"

"Cheaper maintenance," Lumberjack said.

"But it's still a Jaguar," Vaughn insisted. "Talk about class personified."

"Personified?" smiled Lumberjack.

"Don't be dense, Bradley."

"Although I suppose," Dix was rambling, "that even with the change under the hood, the Jaguar's outward combination of phallic streamlining, convertible top and overall penile redness must prove an irresistible aphrodisiac to female homo sapiens."

"Hell," Rupert piped in, "even a ugly dude be getting babes to ride with him in that vehicle."

"That's what I just said."

Vaughn finally completed his salad masterpiece.

"Thanks, guy," he said to Lumberjack.

As Vaughn headed for the wait station, I stuck my arm out and planted myself in his way.

"Got a ticket for that, Bert?"

"Yes, sir, right here. Uno employee salado." He showed me his charge ticket. I kicked aside a stray french fry and pointed to a wooden seam in the scuffed vinyl floor where the kitchen had been added on to the renovated woodframe house.

"See this here line? You're in my realm."

"Oh, come on, Lee. I came here straight from my show and didn't have a chance to grab any chow. I didn't want to put you guys to any trouble."

I rubbed my thumb and forefinger together.

"See this? World's smallest violin."

"You don't own this kitchen, 'Captain Hobart.'"

THE EXTINCTION OF RHINOS IN MEXICO

"The name's Iceman."

"Oh right. Since when?"

"Vaughn, soon as you get back here and scrub pots and pans and cook and get all hot and sticky and smelly, you can share the same benefits as us, including the nickname of your choice."

"Oh grow up. You'd best not smart off to Tully today. He's not in the mood for it."

"Aw, did he frown at you?"

"I was in this morning for java, and he was on the rag about the missing—" he caught himself, suddenly realizing and relishing the fact that he knew some gossip I didn't.

"Let me guess," I said. "He was upset about your missing brain?"

"Let's just say I wouldn't be so cocky if I were you."

"Let's just say if you were me I'd kill myself."

"You don't know everything, Lee. I've got the skinny on this."

"Wake me when I'm impressed."

I let him pass and spiked his ticket. You got to nip these things in the bud, so I went back to have a little heart to heart with L-jack. He was plastic wrapping the salads. I got in his face close enough for him to count the blackheads on my nose.

"If he's your boyfriend, I won't say nothing more."

"He's not."

"Nah, I'm serious. If y'all are lovers, I won't interfere."

His face turned the color of a cherry tomato as he started a new batch of dinner salads, tossing the little salad bowls out on the counter the way a dealer does cards at a poker game.

"I can handle a twoway street," I said. "But that pendejo don't play fair."

"Look, this is a restaurant kitchen, not Mission Control."

That was a little below the belt and I chewed on it a moment, careful to keep eye contact locked in while I readjusted my bandana. I wear it tied as a headband the way David Carradine does on *Kung Fu*. The original one, I mean. Ever since they got the old episodes syndicated on cable Sunday mornings, I've tried not to miss it. It's like my church.

"Point is," I said softly, "he wants us to do him favors, only he don't do jackshit for us."

Lumberjack shifted his eyes to the salads. I could tell he got the message.

"Everything's some big deal with you."

"Heck yeah!" I hooted. "Want to make something of it?"

He looked at me and caught the sarcasm and shook his head with a crooked smile. I bumped the volume on the radio up a notch.

We cooked hard and fast. It's like a greasy ballet, Bert, except that instead of Stravinsky by an orchestra you have Def Leppard on the tubemeister. Between that, the chingada dumbwaiter, the jet turboruckus of the giant exhaust fan over our heads, and the rattlyass air conditioner that sounded like an old tractor, you had to yell just to tell a secret. Beef fat spattering, butter sizzling, peanut oil boiling—the air's a sludge of hot grease. The pure noise and speed of all that food cooking is a headrush, Bert.

"Help me, Mis-ter Wi-zard," I called.

El Jack laughed. He knew I was just joking about needing help. He laughed whenever I cracked a joke. Lumberjack laughed easy. Too easy. For my thinking he was just a little too jolly to be on the safe side.

I turned my attention to the tickets up across the window. "Let's see, we got salmon. Salmon. Salmon. And oh, here's one for salmon. Something's fishy here."

Rupert took the plastic tub from the cooler under the Line.

"Salmon alert," he said. "I need three more to finish these orders."

THE EXTINCTION OF RHINOS IN MEXICO

"Lumberjack! I will gladly pay you Tuesday for that fish today!"

He brought the fish up packed in ice.

"Behind you, Iceman."

"That's what scares me."

He stashed the fish in the line cooler, then began restocking the Line with pickles, tomato slices, jícama, sprouts and olives.

"You've been working here about a month," I said.

"Just about. What, do I get a party?"

"I'll handle the jokes, Lumberjack. You think you can handle the Line?"

"I'm a prep cook. That's all I want."

"Mighty unambitious for a Nam vet college boy."

"If it's any of your business."

"You must think you're pretty smart, helping Rachel study."

He flushed. "I told y'all, it's not like that."

"But you'd like it to be, wouldn't you?"

"She asked me. Look, she's trying to better herself."

"You saying there's something wrong with her the way she is?"

"No. But she doesn't want to be a waitress the rest of her life."

"Maybe she don't want to be saved neither."

He looked at me. "Just because you're happy where you are, don't try to hold her here."

"And I guess you expect me to just buy that your motivations are pure."

"I like her. She knows that."

I stared him down. "Lumberjack. I don't want nobody in my kitchen who can't handle things. Everything. Now get me some Go boxes. And none of your lollygaggin'. I mean it."

He went to the wait station, where the styrofoam To Go

containers were stacked to the ceiling on top of the ice machine. Rachel came in and poked him in the ribs.

"Alright, Mr. KnowItAll, what's Pi Kappa Alpha?"

"Sounds like a sorority."

I made a rude buzzer noise. "Wrong! Get back to work. You failed this question."

He went back to taking styrofoam go containers down.

"What do I get if I know?" I asked Rachel.

"Can't you ever just give a simple answer?"

"Rachel, there ain't none of those."

She aboutfaced to leave.

"It's Tully's frat," I said. "Why?"

She came back and put her face in the window. "I was passing by the office and heard Tully chewing somebody out."

"Who?"

"Who else was in his fraternity?"

"I guess you're going to have to tell me."

"I don't know either," she lied. "The door was mostly shut and I didn't think that much about it. Only I heard him say 'If you weren't Pi Kappa Alpha I'd throw you to the sharks.' Or wolves. Something like that."

Something like that. But definitely not the truth, the whole truth and nothing but the truth. She picked up her two armloads of plates and loaded them into the dumbwaiter. Since El Jack was rubbernecking Rachel instead of watching what he was doing, he wound up pulling down the whole stack of styrofoam containers off the ice machine and onto the floor right as Tully walked in. As Lumberjack scurried to pick them up, Rachel pinched his butt and he jumped.

"Hey!"

"I couldn't resist."

"I was afraid it was Tully."

Tully smiled in protest, shaking his head. "Isn't that just the way it is? Suck one dick and you're a queer."

Tully Metzger was a laid back yup; duck footed, handsome and growing out. Every year he added a new ring of fat, like some walking talking live oak tree. The waitrons always had to dodge around him. The place could be burning down and Tully would be moseying through, checking on things and spouting orders. The man got off to being owner. And so long as the food came out fast and beautiful, Tully was partial to weird kitchens.

"You!" Rachel poked Tully in the chest angrily. "Stay away from Lily."

Lumberjack brought me the containers. He kept an eye on Rachel.

Tully had the innocent look down. "What are you talking about?"

"I know where your priorities lie," Rachel said. "Between the new girl's legs."

Rupert got a kick out of that one. He stirred the new batch of chicken fried gravy he was fixing.

"What happened to innocent until proven guilty?" says Tully.

"How many times equals proof?"

"Rakey, you don't have the jurisdiction anymore." He said it gently.

"She don't have the *dick*, that's for sure," Rupert said to me.

Rachel turned away from Tully and bowed her head over the paper lace doilies. The other waitrons worked around her.

"Tully, what is she? Seventeen?"

Seventeen? Bert, who did she think she was talking to? At Easter me and Steve and Tully had driven down to the border. We was drinking margaritas in a Boy's Town bar where everything looked like it had been painted over with week-old dishwater. Some putas were calling at us in Spanish from another table. Tully's digging it even though he don't understand a word. Even though I'm a Reyes, I can't understand much more. They paddled us at school if we talked mex. My dad used to take off his belt if I talked it at home. Said it was unAmerican.

A matching set comes over who're still under warranty. Can't be more than 12 or 13, max.

"You boys want to have?" the littlest one asks Tully.

"You're too ugly."

Steve hands the first one twenty bucks to show her nips. Tully shakes his head.

"Lee," he says to me, "what's worse than a California earthquake?"

Who ain't heard that one, Bert? But he yanks a Texas titty twister on the kid. She yelps. She's pissed off, both girls are pissed off and start spitting chingas at us. Tully sends them away. I buy us more margaritas. Tully buys us two fourteen year olds. They look like they have less mileage on them than the first girls. We share them in a tidy room in the back that smells of Lysol mopped over piss and pussy and old booze vomit. Ah, romance.

Rachel hurried out of the wait station. Tully stuck his head through the order window, never minding that the waitrons were forced to work around him.

"I thought I told you to keep the radio down to a roar," he said.

"What'd ya say?"

Tully shook his head. "Know the difference between a blowjob and a hamburger?" he asked.

"No."

"Hey, then let's do lunch."

Rupert laughed.

"I'd love to give you a chuckle on that one, Jefe," I said, yanking a chicken-fried steak from the fryer. "But I'll have to get back to you. I'm a little pressed for time."

"What's the problem?"

"The problem is, I should be out enjoying myself and

THE EXTINCTION OF RHINOS IN MEXICO

instead I'm in here cooking my ass off," Rupert says.

"Big Max is missing in action," I reported.

"I know," Tully said, taking a french fry off one of the plates and popping it into his mouth. "I fired him."

Rupert looked over at me.

"Some money was missing from the office," Tully said.

"How much money?"

"Twenty five hundred."

I whistled. "So how come I never heard nothing about it?"

"It was all over and done with pretty quick."

"Did you get it back?"

"Not yet. I talked to a police detective, though. Problem is, we don't have any smoking gun evidence."

"Slight detail."

Stacy's smothered steak was ready, so I plated it and the chickenfried, slung some fries and pulled the ticket right about the time she dashed in.

"You did the order! Thank you! Bless you! You saved my life!"

"I helped too," Rupert said.

"Love thy tip jar as thyself," I told her, pointing it out to her since she used it so rarely. "Large denominations not refused."

"I'll catch you later," she said breathlessly, and then was gone.

"Promises, promises," Rupert said.

Tully chuckled and sauntered back to the prep table, where Lumberjack was cutting beef tenderloin on the big circular blade electric slicer. I pretended like I needed something from under the prep counter so I could accidentally on purpose overhear them.

Tully reached up and turned the radio down.

"How come you've got this up so loud?" he looked at Lumberjack challengingly. El Jack glanced past Tully down at me and I shook my head.

"I didn't notice."

"Well wake up and live."

Now I know Tully and that tone and even though he chuckled, he was making a serious point. A lot of people get the wrong idea about Tully because he comes off as such an easy going dude.

Back in the fall, Tully had taken Steve the bartender, me and Big Max to Tully's lease down in Duval county. Main reason was he wanted to show off his newest acquisition, a Mossman Streetsweeper. It's like a tommygun only it fires shotgun shells.

"People call you Sir when you have one of these," said Steve.

We took turns trying it out. It was a blast to shoot. The thing is gas powered, which keeps it from bucking too bad. The place to be was behind Big Max. He didn't want to actually kill anything, he just loved to shoot. Me, I'm the other way around. I've got too much of a killing instinct. One time I went night hunting, and without hardly thinking, I drilled a jackrabbit on the run at 100 yards with only headlights for light. So I discipline myself mentally, like the Kung Fu masters, to keep my instinct in check.

We hadn't seen no real wildlife that afternoon, anyway, so we just obliterated rabid trees, vicious beer cans and wild bottles. Then we run across a cluster of armadillos chowing down on some juicy grubs.

Tully chunks a rock to scare the critters. They scatter, wobbling for the barbed wire fence where the cactus and underbrush would hide them.

"Let's see how many can make it to the fence," Tully says, casually bringing the streetsweeper to bear.

"Hey, no," Big Max says.

Tully lets the critters run until they get just about to the safety of the fence.

Then he opens up. It was like that scene near the end of

THE EXTINCTION OF RHINOS IN MEXICO

The Wild Bunch, only with armadillos.

Tully's a very sharing person; he lets Steve go for it next. Pretty quick there's only one armadillo left. Sudden quiet in the countryside. My ears are ringing. Big Max has tears in his eyes. Tully grabs the streetsweeper from Steve, and sticks it into my hands so I can get in on the fun. I open my mouth, but can't get out nothing smart fast enough. So Tully yanks the weapon from me, walks over and lets her rip. So close the burst blows the fugitive to dillo shrapnel. Now I've heard that the streetsweeper was designed as a riot control gun. Bert, you won't catch me at the revolution if the Man is toting toys like that.

Wading through the casualties, Steve finds one that's gory, but still thrashing. Big Max stares at it like he's going to cry. Seeing the mangled body flopping around, I feel a little queasy myself. Tully walks over with his Luger and fires down on it.

"Mercy killing," he smiles.

Now where was I?

Oh yeah, so Tully reached over and picked a sliver of the meat from the slicer and ate it.

"Delicious. You smoke this, Brad?"

"No, I'm tryin' to quit."

Tully grinned. "I see Lee's already rubbing off on you. Well, you cooked it just right."

"I'm catching onto things."

"Think you're ready for the Line?"

"I'm happy where I am."

"Are you? I think you're too sharp to just prep. Waste of my money. Look, Big Max is history. I need a replacement, a guy with a head on his shoulders."

"I don't want the pressure."

Tully massaged Brad's lumberjack shoulders like a boxer's trainer.

"It's not that hard. You'll pick it up fast. Be a regular J.

Alfred Frycook in no time."

Lumberjack laughed at that. Tully studied him.

"She's not the sharpest tool in the shed, is she?" Tully asked.

"Who?"

"I hear you're tutoring Rachel."

"What, was an announcement published?"

"Take it from me, she just doesn't have the brains for college."

"That's the way you like your girls, isn't it?"

Tully smiled thinly. "You know her mother's in a Louisiana penitentiary for murder. Gutted her husband with a knife."

That made Lumberjack's gears turn. "That why you dumped her?"

"Caveat emptor, that's all," Tully shrugged. He saw the look on El Jack's face and knew he'd hit a nerve. "Come on, Brad, what are you thinking—marriage, kids?" Tully said this in a gentle tone. It hit me that Tully actually wanted Lumberjack to be his friend.

"Given her brainpower," Tully went on, "if she was ugly, would you be sniffing around her? Imagine yourself married to her for fifteen years. Three kids, a mortgage. Do you two talk about anything? Anything you can stand?"

Stacy barged into the wait station all in a tizzy and holding a plumber's helper.

"Tul-ly, the ladies bathroom is stuck up again."

"Kind of like someone we all know," I said.

Tully grabbed the plumber's helper, held it up like a sword and looked back at us.

"Another executive decision," he said, then plunged through Door Number 1. Rupert was dipping a spoonful of his fresh gravy.

"Say, MacIntyre, come on over here and have a taste," he said. "This'll make your dick hard."

Lumberjack looked all thoughtful and serious when he

THE EXTINCTION OF RHINOS IN MEXICO

came over and sampled the creamy gravy. He complimented Rupert on how good it was.

"Of course it is. It's *good* to be cook," said Rupert. He nudged El Jack. "Say, she's on the plump side."

"Mm."

"I like 'em that way. Yes sir. She a natural blonde?"

"I told you, man."

Rupert twisted his mouth funny. "You don't fool me, White Boy."

Lumberjack retreated to the prep table.

"I seen the way you eye that bitch," called Rupert. "Personally, I think you're just holding out on me and the Iceman."

Lumberjack said nothing, just went back to the table and prepped quietly.

"Now what did I say?" Rupert asked.

"Take the helm," I told him, sliding a finished order into the window and pulling the ticket.

"What do you think I *been* doing while you guys were back there jawin'?"

Outside the restaurant in the damp sea breeze, you could smell the grease on yourself. Renegade firecrackers popping off in the distance. Tully's sleek red Jag was parked next to my El Camino out near the alley.

It had been almost two weeks since Tully had eightysixed Rachel. A week ago I had got off work and around his car in the dark I seen some yellow patches. It was them post it note papers on the ground in a ring around the car. I picked one up. When you look at someone's chicken scratchings forty someodd times a night on order tickets, you come close to being a handwriting expert. In a pretty looking lady's writing were the words "I'm sorry." It was Rachel's hand. Every one of the papers said the same thing.

That same night I drove my El Camino north along Ocean Drive, then west from the bay past downtown and got on the

Crosstown Expressway, Hendrix on my tape deck drainoing the grease out of my brain. Only a few cars were prowling at that hour and none of them got in my way. I cruised the Crosstown around the loop and kept going out along South Padre Island Drive until it ran out on the way to Flour Bluff and became just a divided roadway with stoplights.

I turned off by a weathered bait shop that also sold shells and tourist t-shirts. I drove down the lane of old one story asbestos siding houses with sandy yards and oleanders and scrawny tallow trees. Nobody had ever poured any sidewalks out here. Still just the grassy drainage ditches and oyster shell driveways.

After I knock, she peers through the curtain, then answers the door in a bathrobe. The tv's on. No sidewalks, but they have cable now.

"It's a little late," Rachel says. Her eyes red from crying.
"Thought you might need some company."
"That's sweet. But not tonight, Sugar."

Like Rupert said, I retrieve them. I flash a baggie of pot and say "The mosquitoes are kind of feisty tonight."

She unhooks the screen door to let me in. She takes the baggie and we sit on the ratty couch in front of the tv while she manicures the pot on a tip tray using a wallet photo of her family. There's a Mademoiselle magazine and a copy of *TAXI* on the coffee table. Also two green wine bottles, empty, and two goblets. There's blood colored wine and a cigarette butt in the glass with lipstick on the rim. The other one has crusting, dried wine in the bottom.

"Where's Debba Lynn?" I ask, peering around.
"She's been staying over at Bart's and Hooter's."
Perfect.
"The Bandido dudes?"
"Yeah."

We took a couple of hits off her bong.
"You and her have another knockdown dragout?"

"No, they've been partying for two or three days."
I chuckle at that image.
"They make a lovely couple and a half."
"I don't ask personal questions, Cher."
"Good policy. So you in the market for a new roommate?"
"No."
"No harm in asking."
"You could help me with my homework."
"That's more Lumberjack's style."
"He kind of likes me, doesn't he?" She smiles, pleased with herself.
"And boiling oil's kind of hot."
"He's really a gentleman."
"Lot of folk been screwed by that breed."
The smile drains out her.
"On the other hand," I chirp, "Ol' Lumberjack does seem awful earnest."
She looks so sad that I touch her cheek.
"You want me to kiss you?" I asked.
"Sugar, you better just do it and don't talk."
I lean in and kiss her soft round cheek, then her lips and her neck just behind her ear. She sighs and shudders. I smell the wine and marijuana. I fumble with the buttons of her shirt, trying not to bust off any.
"You make love like you're fixin' a carburetor," she murmurs, swaying a little. Well I never claimed to be Casanova, though I am pretty decent at repairing cars. She lays over then and is asleep. I don't know why, but I stop. Any other gal and I go ahead and do the deed. Instead, I reach out and stroke her blonde hair, I hold it and draw it through my knifenicked, burn callused hands. Her hair feels smooth, soothing, like corn silk. I watch her for a long time, watch her sleeping and I'm thinking about all we've been through over the years, me, her and Tully. First San Antonio, then Dallas, now back here on the coast where I grew up. Not important

things to the world, but our times, the shared laughs and troubles and yearnings. And now Tully and her are on the rocks. Bide your time, I tell myself, and I touch her hair again.

Near dawn I crashed. Dreamed that I was the only cook in a humongous restaurant and people were ordering foods I'd never heard of.

That was almost a week ago, the last time I slept, six days and counting. But I wasn't down yet. I checked my watch. Half past ten on Independence Day night shift. Soon I would have been awake for a week. The kid's going for the record. The crowd roars. Only another hour and a half til shutdown, and then another two for cleanup. I did a snootful of crystal and went back inside restaurant.

A late monsoon of tickets. People out celebrating Firecracker Day. I cooked, Rupert cooked, Lumberjack prepped, Dix ran dishes through the Hobart, full tilt. And still we wasn't fast enough. It got to that kind of busy where you don't think, you just *do*. Got to where you felt like your sweat couldn't get out because the coating of grease on you was stopping up the pores.

Six days and counting. Closing in on one solid week.

Time gets weird in a Saturday night rush. A cook has to keep a lot of things in his head, look ahead, see what's coming, remember what's gone by so he'll know if he's about to run out of something. Timing's everything. It's like being the plate spinner on Captain Kangaroo.

"Take no prisoners!" I hollered, feeling the crank and a new wave of adrenaline kick in.

We had the grill, the broiler, the oven, every stove burner and all the fryers loaded and cranked to warp speed. Rachel had started sneaking shots of vodka in the wait station until she was falling behind.

"Rachel, don't let him get to you," Lumberjack was telling her.

"Cher, just another couple of slugs, and I'll be immune."

THE EXTINCTION OF RHINOS IN MEXICO

"Come on, don't. Please."

"Don't tell me what to do."

Finally he walked away from her. The other waitrons kept slapping tickets down, orders, more orders.

The back door slammed open.

"Max!" cried Rachel, drunkhappy. Big Max stood in the open doorway like the longlost Yeti.

"Yahta-hey!" he shouted, and hugged Rachel. Max had this sweet voice and the face of a baby on top of a six foot six, slope shouldered, pear shaped frame. Weighed a quarter ton and was half a bubble off plumb. He looked at Rachel.

"You're drunk."

"I'm pissed," she said.

"Then you've got say it," Max told her. El Jack dropped a couple of orders of fries into the fryer basket. Next to Big Max, even El Jack looked kind of scrawny.

"Say what?" she asked.

"Say *Bohunk green, sewing machine.*"

"What for?"

"Just say it. Bohunk green, sewing machine."

"What does it mean?"

"Nothing."

"It doesn't mean something?"

"Nothing at all. Come on, say it. Bohunk green, sewing machine."

"I'll say it," said Lumberjack. "Bohunk green, sewing machine." This tickled Rachel and she laughed.

"See? Don't you feel better?" he asked Lumberjack. "I do." The hornrim glasses Big Max wore disguised the threat of his eyes by making him look like a kid. He had always wore a Hawaiian print shirt instead of the white ones the rest of us wore.

"Hey, you should've seen the fireworks over the bay," Big Max said.

"We heard Tully fired your Yankee Doodle ass," said

Rupert.

"Oh he did. Yesterday. Absolutely without justification." Max got a fond faraway look on his face. "The fireworks show," he said, "was a spectacle beyond mere jingoism."

Max turned to me. "Say it, Captain Hobart."

"Think I'll pass."

"Come on, sticks and stones and all that."

"I'm tryin' to cook here you big galoot."

"You fucking better say it right now."

He pushed his face into mine, just the way my dad used to and I felt like running away, felt the old panic, just like I used to. My heart was hammering. Only I wasn't running no more. With a shaky hand I reached back behind me, my hand found my chopping knife, and my fingers closed on the haft. If he kept it up...

Suddenly Lumberjack stood between me and the giant.

"I'll say it again, Max," he said. "Bohunk green, sewing machine." He said it like it was the easiest thing in the world. Max pounded on El Jack's broad shoulders.

"I knew you'd say it, Brad. A cleancut, All American youth like yourself ought to raise up your voice in hosannas to the Lord for giving you those shoulders."

El Jack couldn't help but grin. "So what's up, man?" he asked.

"Came for my radio. You sure you're not wearing shoulder pads?"

El Jack and Rachel laughed.

"No, I'm serious."

"Jack here laughs at everything," I said.

"I laughed too," said Rachel.

Big Max raised Lumberjack's arm and took a big whiff of his pit. "Ah, I love the smell of a Christian."

"What are you talking about?" asked Rachel. She was a bit of a Baptist herself.

"I'm not a Christian," Lumberjack said.

"Really? Are you sure?"

"Brad, I can't believe you'd deny our Lord." Rachel was staring at Lumberjack.

"Yeah, you're so . . . nice, such an upstanding geebhowick, I figured you had to be a Bible thumper," said Max.

"What are you then?"

"Why do I have to be anything?"

Max turned to Rachel. "My God, don't you see? It has to be suppressed sexual energy."

"Quit taking the Lord's name in vain," Rachel frowned.

"I don't think young Master Bradley has ever been laid. He's well read, well traveled, but unfucked."

"Ah," nodded Dix. "Hence, abundant laughter."

"Didn't you never even go to Boys Town?" I asked El Jack. "Never? What about Nam? All that poon tang?"

"Nam," muttered Rupert, shaking his head. "Shit."

"Son, you're just naive and repressed," Big Max said to him. "Look at that face, Rachel. Don't you just want to give him a big old kiss?"

"Not really," she giggled.

"Cut it out, Max." Lumberjack wasn't chuckling no more.

Big Max reached around and grabbed El Jack's face by the cheeks with his big paw, squeezing so that Lumberjack's lips puckered. Drunk as she was, Rachel couldn't help but laugh at the sight. Lumberjack knocked Max's arm away.

"Fuck you," said El Jack.

"Not me."

"Talk to Vaughn," I said.

This whole time Rupert has kept right on cooking. Now he scooted past us and went to the slicer with a tenderloin. The old tubemeister radio on the shelf above his head pumped out some Metallica.

"Shut up, you guys," Rachel said, still laughing. She put her hand on Lumberjack's shoulder. "I'm sorry for laughing."

She got serious. "Really, you believe that Jesus was our

Saviour, don't you?"

Lumberjack looked like he was about to bite her head off. This time it was Big Max who laughed with that kid kind of enthusiasm that his big size made so dangerous.

"Screw what he says. Hell, yes Brad's a Christian. He walks the talk." Max slapped him on the back and turned to me. Behind him I saw Vaughn come through Door Number 2, see Max, and do an about face right back out again.

"Time for you to say it, Captain."

No use arguing with the lummox. "Bohunk green, sewin' machine."

Dix came forward carrying two trays of clean glasses.

"I'll say it," he declared, "because it sounds like an incantation. Excuse me. I could use that, because you see, I'm a witch. A white witch without any spells."

He set everything aside and stood ready.

"Bohunk green, sewing machine. Excuse me."

"Your turn, Rupert."

"Holmes, I ain't saying nothin' that weird."

"You better."

"Nuh uh. No sir."

Max moved toward Rupert.

"*Bohunkgreensewingmachine*," Rupert spit out. "You crazy." He kept at the tenderloin, shoving it onto the spinning blade. Slice after slice. Big Max turned around to us and spread his arms.

"That just leaves you, Rachel."

"I don't want to say it," said Rachel. "Leave me alone."

Big Max's face dropped as he gaped at her.

"Aw, then it must've been you, Rachel."

"It wasn't me, Max."

"You took the money. Process of elimination."

I looked at her. She did look guilty about something. At that moment Baron, the old muscley tom cat that Max had adopted, rubbed up against the open door and made a big

THE EXTINCTION OF RHINOS IN MEXICO

meow. Baron spoke up again. Max reached into the Line cooler and broke off part of a raw burger patty. He held it over Baron.

"Say it, Baron. Come on: Bohunk green, sewing machine."

That old gigolo Baron started talking up a storm. Max fed him the burger meat and the cat hunkered down gobbling it. That was Big Max: psycho with a heart of gold.

Rupert kept running back and forth from the Line to the slicer. Some nights seems like the whole population's craving the same food. Like some sort of telepathic hunger connecting us. Some nights it'll be ribeyes, another it'll be chickenfrieds. Tonight we had an early run on sautéed salmon and now it had shifted to cold tenderloin sandwiches with sour cream horseradish sauce.

"HEY!" Tully hollered from over at Door Number 1. "Get that animal out of here!" Vaughn watched from a safe distance as Tully came back.

"He's not an animal," said Big Max, wide eyed. "This is Baron."

"Get out, kitty, go on! Shoo!"

"Don't touch him," Big Max said.

"What are you doing here, Max?" Tully said.

"You owe me my last paycheck."

Tully put his hands on his hips. "No sir, I don't."

Big Max looked down at the floor.

"I didn't take the money," he said. "Rachel did."

"I did not!" She was hot. "Tully, tell him."

Lumberjack was staring at her.

"She didn't take it, Max," Tully said. "I know that for a fact."

"Well it wasn't me either."

Suddenly Tully caught Baron in the ribs with his loafer and the gato was out the door. "Beat it!"

"Son of a bitch," said Max, and he pulled out a footlong flat head screwdriver.

"Max, come on," said Lumberjack. Max slammed the back door shut and dropped the two by four bar across it.

Stacy came into the wait station.

"Stacy, get back!" said Rachel.

"Order in!" Stacy said, ignoring Rachel and looking at us. As she headed out Door Number 2, Big Max moved quickly to block her way.

"Hi, Stacy."

Stacy stopped. She stared at all of us standing there.

"Hello? It's very busy out there."

"Go stand with the others over there," Max ordered.

"Why?" She smiled now, suspecting some prank. "What are y'all up to?"

"Be cool, honey," said Rupert, continuing to cook. "Fool's just robbing the place."

"I'm not robbing it. I just came for my check and my radio."

Steve came pushing through Door Number 1.

"Ladies, the natives are getting restless. Stacy you'd better get your tush out there. Lily just seated you a sixtop."

Big Max put a hand on Steve's shoulder. Steve jumped when he saw who it was.

"Max! Hey buddy, what's happening? What are you doing here?"

Big Max brandished the screwdriver.

"This is a screwup," he said. "Get over there."

Steve backed over to the rest of us.

"You can't keep all of us back here," said Tully. He took the two by four off the back door.

"Man, don't do that!" Max shouted and we all jumped.

"Maybe it's like he said, Tully." Lumberjack wiped his hands on his apron. "Maybe he didn't do it."

"I didn't, man. I wouldn't. My parole officer came by. I need this job," Max said. "My mother..." He broke down blubbering. "If I go back to jail, she'll be out on the street."

THE EXTINCTION OF RHINOS IN MEXICO

Rupert slipped back to the slicer again to cut some more meat.

"Max, this won't do any good," said Lumberjack. "We'll find you a lawyer and get this worked out."

"I'm taking my radio."

Big Max moved to get his radio, but Tully moved faster. He reached above Rupert at the slicer and grabbed the radio with both hands. He yanked it, the cord caught Rupert, who flinched as Tully smashed the tubemeister onto the floor.

Rupert let out a yelp and clutched his hand.

"Oh sweet Jesus."

Dix checked out Rupert.

"Excuse me," said Dix.

"Dix, do you have to do that now?" Stacy said crossly.

"Excuse me but there's been an injury."

Lumberjack went over and checked Rupert's hand.

"I'm afraid to look," said Rupert. "I can't look."

"Then don't look!" Lumberjack growled. He grabbed a rag.

"I'll call EMS," Rachel said and ran out front.

"Get the police here while you're at it," called Tully.

"Okay, Rupert," Lumberjack said while we crowded around, "I'm applying pressure to stop the bleeding."

"Motherfucking Boy Scout," said Rupert.

"Trustworthy, loyal, helpful—"

"—friendly, kind, courteous, yeah, yeah, yeah, I was a scout myself."

"You'll be fine, man," Max was worried for Rupert.

"Max, this is your fault," Tully said.

"You'll be alright, Rupert. You'll be alright," Max said, backing away. "I'm sorry, Rupert. I'm sorry, man. It'll be okay." Then he ambled out the back door and was gone.

I grabbed El Jack some more kitchen rags. He threw off the soggy rag and just before he pressed on the dry ones, I saw Rupert's right hand. He had caught himself between the thumb and index finger. You could see the pink whiteness of the meat and bone inside his black skin just before the blood flooded out over it.

After the EMS had left and the police had left, we sort of cooked on autopilot. Finally, about the time Dix started explaining how come he didn't believe in using deodorant, Lumberjack walked out. Now Dix ain't exactly the King of Conversation, but I knew it wasn't his tacky story that made Lumberjack split. I made sure all my orders were happening, and then went out back too.

Lumberjack was there, on the wooden deck, hands braced on the railing, staring past the full parking lot into the alley. I heard an ambulance roar past on its way to Spohn Hospital a few blocks over. In the distance, sometimes closer, you could hear strings of Black Cats popping off.

"Don't worry, I'm coming back in," he said.

"I ain't worried." I lit a joint and handed it to him. He looked at it, then took it in his fingers, took a big toke and passed it back to me.

"I have this theory," he said while still holding the sweet smoke.

"Uh-oh. You been wearing the Thinking Cap again?" I licked the joint where it was burning unevenly and took a hit. He slowly exhaled a cloud.

"It seems like you ought to be able to rig people genetically to convert light into food the way plants do."

"Yeah, I seen this at the Viking Twin Drive In when I was a kid."

I got a smile out of him on that one.

"Human photosynthesis," said Dr. Lumberstein. "It could be a way to solve the world's hunger problem. It might simplify a lot of things."

"Photosynthesis? Now correct me if I'm wrong, but wouldn't that make us green?"

This time he laughed and took another hit. "Bohunk

green," he said.

"Besides, ain't you overlooking something?"

"What's that?"

"Bright idea like that would put me out of business."

"Well I hadn't thought that far."

"I didn't think so." A stray firecracker went off somewhere. His mind was somewhere else.

"Tully was right," he said. "Rupert's right. Even Big Max was right."

I didn't say nothing for a while.

"Hey, so you like her," I shrugged.

"Do I? It feels like I do, but I'm beginning to suspect I'm just like every other horny prick, only I flatter myself that I'm a nice guy, so I convince myself I'm in love with a woman I really only want to fuck, and go through this ludicrous, tiresome nice guy routine."

"You *have* been to college, ain't you?"

"And now when it's turned out, well I mean I've known for weeks now that she doesn't want me that way, I can't stop feeling like I love her, even though I don't think I even like her anymore."

I nodded. So there it was.

"She's still nuts about Tully." He sounded like he couldn't believe it.

"She's got a loyal heart," I said.

He looked at me until I handed the joint to him.

"But bad judgment," he dragged on it and held it in. I took it back and sucked on it.

"She hung a lot of hopes on the man."

A Lumina left the parking lot and an Olds came in and tried to take its place.

"I don't get love," he said.

"Life's weird, Bert."

"Seems like way too much of a crap shoot."

It took the Olds several tries to maneuver into the narrow space. A couple who couldn't have been out of their twenties got out of the car laughing and walked around to the entrance up front.

"Y'know I'm glad..." I stopped and changed tack. "It's good you've been helping her with summer school. She needed somebody to."

He looked at me, then looked away. I offered him the roach, but he waved his hand. He carefully went back inside. I tapped the roach out against the wood rail and stuck it in the watch pocket of my jeans, looking at Tully's red, red Jaguar. Sirens began screaming.

Next day on the Channel 3 news Stacy caught the story about Max being dead and then it didn't take long for the word to spread. After he had left us Max had walked from the Naples Bar and Grill for two blocks, then stepped out onto Ocean Drive and lay down in the traffic.

Around the Bee and Gee, Vaughn was telling all the customers about how Tully had saved the day. Big Max had grown about a foot taller and a hundred pounds heavier in Vaughn's telling.

"This will make a killer chapter in my autobiography," Vaughn said.

Early the next evening, we were cruising, prepping for the dinner rush. All of us felt a little dazed and were still thinking about Big Max. We'd gone back to the choof old plastic radio with the bent coat hanger antenna and plenty of static. I had Dix making salads and I was lopping the heads off a school of trout. Lumberjack was at the Line fixing a roux for gravy. Tully drove his Jag up out back and bopped in, freshly showered and shaved, cologned and dressed, in a clean gator shirt, khaki slacks and spitshine tasseled loafers.

"Hey," he said. "How come Helen Keller wears skintight pants?"

El Jack hammered the twenty inch skillet down on the

THE EXTINCTION OF RHINOS IN MEXICO

stove. The metal on metal rang an earsplitting warning that stopped everyone in their tracks.

"So you can read her fucking lips!" Lumberjack yelled.

Tully just smiled that smile of his. Lumberjack was panting like he had just run a mile. Reckon he must've been simmering for a while. He was gripping that skillet like he might start swinging it. Shoulders twitching, Lumberjack went over to Tully.

"Hah. Hah. Hah." Lumberjack roared it pointblank into Tully's face.

But I don't think Tully was afraid. His humor just slid right off him and his eyes got like those trout. I slipped over and put my hand on El Jack's chest, pushing him back toward the fryers.

"Hey, Jack, I'm the sarcastic one around here."

"I don't want to see you in here anymore," Tully said to Lumberjack. Rachel rushed into the wait station with a worried face. Apparently she had heard our commotion out front. El Jack looked at her only once and very briefly, then shouldered past us and kicked the back door open with his grease stained work boots. Out in the parking lot he rassled with his apron, ripping the material getting it off. It was practically comical.

Rachel looked shaken. Guess we all were.

That night I got a jump on the cleanup, starting to break down the Line forty five minutes before closing time, storing all the pickles, okra, tomatoes and stuff in plastic containers and working from that. Ran the grease filters through the Hobart. Tully came back and told me I'd be training a new guy Tuesday night. I drained and strained the hot peanut oil from both fryers, poured it back in but left only one of them turned on. By the time midnight rolled around, all I had left to clean was the grill. I took a break.

From the outside, the Naples Bar & Grill still looked the same, though most of the old crew was gone now. But hey,

Bert, that's one of the perks to cooking professionally. You don't get stuck with the same people year after year.

After a couple of waitrons came back from dumpster patrol with their wastebaskets, Baron made an appearance at the open back door, looking for Max.

"Where you been hiding out, you ol' pirate?" I said to him.

He stood there flexing his clawless front paws—he'd once belonged to somebody—looking up at me. He moved his mouth but no sound came out.

"Sorry, Buddy." I went back inside and shut the door.

I took the shortcut on cleaning the grill. Instead of scraping it with the grill brick, I tossed on a scoopful of ice to steam all the hard fry crud loose. Through the steam I watched the ice skate across the hot grill, a fast ride on its own melting.

* * *

I had the day off and decided to go check on Rupert. He lived across the Cut, north of the interstate, up past the old bluff cemetery, not far east of the refineries. You could see one of the plants was flaring off some inefficiency from a tall pipe stack. A Cadillac a minute, my dad liked to say, meaning how many bucks worth of gas was going up in smoke. Thing is, the oil company bean counters figured it would cost them even more in lost revenues to shut down the plant to tweak the system. So they burn it up. That's economics for you. On a night when a dozen flares are flaming up yellow, and the offshore wind blows the stink away, the refineries are wicked fine, the bluewhite lights on the pipelines and tall reactors illuminating the sky like some sparkling, promising city.

At noon in the sun they look like metal carcasses. For twenty three years after he left the Marines, Dad worked out there. When I was fourteen he got me a job where I spent

THE EXTINCTION OF RHINOS IN MEXICO

one whole summer cleaning out the insides of the empty ones of those big cylinder storage tanks. The older workers used to laugh to look down in on me. They'd hammer on the metal roof with their wrenches and it would echo with a hellacious racket. With the sun baking the metal, the temperature inside had to be a hundred and forty, heating all the toxins. So kitchen heat ain't never been nothing to me.

Rupert lived with his mother over off Chipito, down San Juan street in an old wooden shotgun shack painted a bright yellow, with a blue tarpaper roof. She felt fortunate to live close to God's Street Ministry, which operated out of an ancient whitewashed movie theater that had been Nicky's Market for years before the ministry took over.

After fixing me a tall glass of ice tea with lemon and too much sugar, Rupert's mother told me where I might could find him. It was only the next street over, so I walked. As you came down the street, you could see down at the end a Union Pacific engine coasting by, and beyond the tracks the sewage treatment tanks and then the dock warehouses and finally the Harbor Bridge crouched over the water like a steel dinosaur skeleton. African brothers were hanging out in doorways, and from some bar, maybe Mary's Epitome, or Yolanda's, I could hear conjunto music spilling out from a jukebox into the street. The August sky was the color of an old aluminum stew pot and it wasn't even lunchtime yet, but it felt like we were all in the stew with the fire turned up and the lid on.

Inside the Ebony Recreation Spot it was midnight, and it took my eyes a second to get used to it. Everyone gave me the once over. As usual, the Mexicans stuck together, and the brothers kept to themselves. Some vatos huddled at a table in a corner, and a couple of brothers with cuesticks were working the quarter table. They had the Conan arms of longshoremen.

"Iceman! Over here."

I looked again and saw Rupert perched on a stool along

the far end of the bar. He waved me over with his bandaged right hand. We greeted each other with a lefthanded soul brother handshake.

"What up, Ice?"

"Ain't nothin' to it."

"You still in the runnin'?"

"Seven days plus. I might never sleep again."

He shook his head. "You are one crazed Mexican."

"How's the paw?"

"Won't be throwing no jabs for a while." He pretended like he was boxing for a minute, then went back to his Schlitz Malt Liquor, lefthanded.

"That blade cut something in my hand so's I can't hardly bend it. Still hurts like a motherfucker, too."

"What's the doctor say?"

"Fuck what that asshole says. He keeps saying to me that he don't like doing workman's comp cases because they don't get well as fast. Right to my face. Like I want to be maimed."

"Just keep working that hand."

"That's what El Jack said."

"You seen him?"

"Last Thursday. He dropped by and met my mama. Know what that boy told me? Said Rupert is German for Robert. I said Aw hell. You telling me that all this time I been a *Bob*?"

Rupert said it with a flat Kansas City whitebread accent that got me chuckling.

"Told me he quit the B and G," said Rupert.

"Fired, more like."

"Shit, that's the last we'll see of *that* white boy."

We both laughed, and then Rupert drank on his Schlitz.

"Hell," he said, "White folks have a way with success. Me, I don't know nothing but cooking and fucking."

"Them's the top two in my book."

"I miss it."

THE EXTINCTION OF RHINOS IN MEXICO

"Cooking or fucking?"

He snickered and slapped my palm with his good hand.

"Thank the Lord it was just my hand that got cut. You know I've had a lady or two threaten other parts with a knife."

"If you'd just take care of business..."

"Oh, I was takin' care of it, only the ladies found out about each other." He smirked and sipped his malt liquor. "Say, tell the truth now. You got a thing for Rachel, yourself, ain't you? Kind of sweet on her, ain't you?"

I shrugged. He studied a while, but let me slide. He raised his bandaged hand for the barkeep. "Brother, bring me another bull over here. Malt liquor bull. Does it every time, the commercial says. What, I still don't know." He laughed at his own joke.

The man brought the bottle and I paid for it.

"This one's on me."

Rupert elbowed me. "Ice, you alright for a cockyass Mexican."

"Don't get all weepy on me."

"I'll kick your ass and we'll see who's crying."

We drank and after a while I got to thinking about the Luger under the seat of my Dad's Toronado. He had showed it to me once before she divorced him. He kept it there for Mom, in case she ever fooled around on him. And all the while he was fucking that checker at the Kmart. He still keeps it there for Mom, just in case he ever finds her. Still, even though she's living in Port Lavaca now.

"My father's a pistol and I'm a sonuvagun," I said out loud.

"You ain't that tough."

I looked at Rupert. "You think you could take me? I mean, look me in the eye and kill me?"

"Now what kind of fool question is that?"

"My dad's the only guy I ever knew that killed someone face to face. In Nam."

"What about Lumberjack?"

"What about him?"

"He *claims* he was over there."

"He might've shot some gooks, but I got a feeling he never stuck a bayonet in one and twisted it."

"Never had to ice anybody myself. No sir. Hope I never have to, 'cause a nigger can't get away with nothin'."

I waited for him to chuckle, but he just gazed at the cold sweat trickling off his bottle.

"Yeah, you got it rough sittin' around here."

"No, I'm serious. They don't call you nigger anymore, they just make you feel like one. Shit, Iceman, what am I going to do if I can't get back into the swing of things? Ain't no way nobody's going to give a nigger high school dropout any money."

Couldn't argue with him there, so we ordered another round and I paid for that too. Me and him was buddies all afternoon.

That night I drove around to the Naples after closing time. The parking lot was empty except for Tully's Jaguar, Steve's pickup and Rachel's Toyota. The back door was locked, but the lights were still bright in back, and the door wasn't barred, so I let myself in through the kitchen with my key. It was clean and the crew gone. I went to see what was behind Door Number 1.

Out front some tasteful excuse for jazz was playing softly over the system and the lights were low. Over at a dark corner of the copper bar I could see Rachel doing a slow grind on Tully's lap as he sat on a bar stool. She was simultaneously leaning across the bar kissing Steve the bartender. They all three laughed at something.

Steve saw me then and came over. He hustled me back through the swinging door into the kitchen.

"What are you doing here, amigo?" he asked. "It's your day off."

"Guess you could say I'm a glutton for punishment."

THE EXTINCTION OF RHINOS IN MEXICO

He leaned in confidentially. "Well listen, two's company, three's a gang bang."

I stared at him for a long moment. "What's the deal; where's Lily?"

Steve went over to the back door and opened it for me.

"She went home with cramps. It's her period."

"Oh, I get it. Tully needs a substitute tonight."

"Be a sport, Hobart."

He hustled me out the back and locked the door behind me. I heard him lay the two-by-four across the door. I stood there grinding my gears for a minute. See, Bert, my philosophy's a combo of Kung Fu and Andy Griffith, with a little Three Stooges thrown in. So ultimately I had to go back in.

I unlocked the front door quiet as a commando.

Tully was whispering some lie into Rachel's ear. He had that worldbytheballs smile he always seemed to be wearing.

"You doing alright, Rachel?" I asked.

They looked around. Tully spread his hands and smiled.

"Fuck you, Lee, I'm telling a joke."

"Maybe I know it already."

"What's the difference between a young whore and an old whore?"

"I give up," Rachel said.

"Young whore uses vaseline," I said. "The old whore uses Dentugrip."

Rachel burst into laughter, which made Steve laugh too. Tully slowly clapped his hands.

"I've got one," she said.

Looking at me, Tully shoved Rachel's empty glass toward Steve. She was already three sheets to the wind.

"Fix Rachel another G and T."

She leaned back against Tully and looked at me from under half closed eyes. The material had bunched on her white buttondown blouse and through an opening I could see the full flesh curve of her right breast, bare under the blouse. I knew she would do anything for Tully to take her back.

"Did y'all know the human brain itself doesn't have any pain sensors?" she said.

"I don't believe I've heard this one," Steve said.

"If you cut your hand or get run over or someone stabs you in your heart, the pain's really all just in your head."

"I missed the joke," said Steve.

"I thought it was funny," Rachel pouted. "Brad told me that once."

"Lumberjack wouldn't know funny if he fell in it," said Tully.

"Mr. Encyclopedia," Steve said. "Good riddance." He laughed through his manicured beard.

"Upsey daisy," said Tully. He hefted Rachel up onto the bar and she lay back on the bar and it made me think of Max lying in the road.

"Maybe you should get some fresh air, Rachel," I said.

"Go get your own toy," said Steve, already starting to feast, kissing on her and unfastening buttons.

Rachel looked up at me. "I'm feelin' no pain, Sugar. No pain whatsoever."

"Look, I'll take you home." I pulled her into a sitting position. She yanked away. She's a surprisingly strong gal.

"Don't! Makin' me dizzy."

I almost got her off the bar.

"Hey, don't go yet," said Tully, using his earnest voice on her.

"Rakey," I said. "You don't have to do this."

"Hit the road, goddamn it." Tully's tone told me the hole I was digging was getting deeper by the second.

She covered her ears with her hands. "Don't take the Lord's name like that. You're not my father, Lee. You can't tell me what to do. I'm not going with you, *Hobart*." She giggled hysterically.

THE EXTINCTION OF RHINOS IN MEXICO

I took her arm. "Then I'll get you a cab. We're leaving."

"The hell you are," Steve said.

"You heard her," said Tully. "Shove off."

She looked at me like a defiant kid.

"Yeah. Shove off." She lifted her nose, planting a cigarette in her mouth. A lighter appeared in Steve's bartender hand and he lit her Camel with professional smoothness and I saw his gold fraternity ring. Funny, I'd never noticed it before.

"I'm havin' a lot of fun now." She blew out smoke.

"Rachel, Tully doesn't give a shit about you."

"That's a lie," he said.

She looked at all of us uncertainly.

"Lie . . . I need to lie down." She pulled away from me and sank down on the copper bar, all but passed out. Tully and Steve had her panties off and her dress up. Steve took his shirt off and was unzipping his pants.

"Rachel," I said.

"Come on, Lee," said Tully, his voice silky. "Just a little midnight snack. She doesn't mind. Here. You go first. Be my guest. Start with some hair taco."

Life's weird, Bert. He raised her dress and there she was. Blonde. Natural blonde. Jesus. Did she want it? I know I did. No. No, she had decided to keep her mouth shut about what she had overheard and in the end Big Max had died for it, really, and she knew that. So here we were. This had become clear the moment I seen Steve's ring. But I don't believe in nothing unless it's scientifically proven.

"Y'know —"my vocal chords betrayed me and I had to clear my throat—"if y'all weren't Pi Kappa Alpha, I'd have to throw you to the sharks."

It had just been a stab in the dark, but when they stopped in mid lick I knew I had them.

I got Rachel home and put her in her own bed. I was out on my feet. Every time I nodded off I saw those dead eyes,

Max's and Tully's... and then I had just cleaned the grill, polished it so that it shined. Then I turned around and it was dirty all over again, crusted with bits of charred fleshy things stuck to it. I started crying and that startled me awake. It had just been a second. Technically I hadn't really gone to sleep.

Sitting huddled on a sand dune, out on Mustang Island, I watched the sky pinken over the gulf, and then I could crawl into my El Camino and sleep at last.

The sun was headed back down when I woke up hot and thirsty. I bought a Tall Boy at the Maverick Market and then drove back along the JFK causeway to Flour Bluff, turning off by the weathered bait shop that also sold tourist curios. I drove down the lane of old one story asbestos siding houses with sandy yards and sweet blossoming oleanders and scrawny tallow trees.

The old armchair and the ratty sofa sat wasted out in the grassy ditch. I opened the screen door and walked in. Her house was hollow sounding and empty except for the usual dirt left behind.

* * *

A few weeks into September I woke up one steamy afternoon and someone had stole my brain and put a piece of stale popcorn in its place, thinking I wouldn't notice. The old rack monster was sitting on me and wouldn't let me out of bed. But I ain't the kind of guy to take life lying down, so I forced myself out of bed and drove me down to the Galleon, the next restaurant I was working at by that time.

Rupert phoned me there, which wasn't all that cool since I was still new kid on the block, but he just had to give me the latest. Seems when Tully had locked up the night before, he had went out to his Jaguar and when he unlocked it, out skedaddled old Baron and a couple of his piss buddies. They

THE EXTINCTION OF RHINOS IN MEXICO

had been locked in the car (windows cracked) for the whole hot sunny day with about ten pounds of sunbaked fishheads.

Another year, another day, another rush. More orders than you can shake a stick at. I've got Rancid jackhammering the guitar on the tape deck to keep me awake. Nine days and counting this time, Bert. A new personal best. Some of the waitrons swear it was Max's ghost that done it. Rupert had a hunch it was Lumberjack. I guess looking back on it, I liked working with Lumberjack about the best. Most people talk about what music they like or their all-time greatest farts. Not Jack. Ever once in a while I still ponder about human photosynthesis. But very rarely do I ever stop to wonder whatever happened to Max's invalid, senile mother.

I'm platespinning now. Do it do it do it the pressure and heat go on forever and ever so you don't bother trying to see way to the long long end just let go and fall into the pulse. They say if you stay up long enough you start to hallucinate, which if you think about it, is dreaming while you're awake. Me, I don't believe in nothing unless it's scientifically proven.

7

CARRION BIRDS

He stands at the hurricane fence again, outside looking in at the planes like at a zoo, feral machine noises etched into his psyche when he could scarcely toddle and his parents carried him to live within a stone's throw of Love Field. He's grown up at the fence now, or is it just that he's always felt grown up, even as a child? Looking as he always looks, peering through the wire diamonds of the fence, tasting the galvanized links with his curling tongue, the metallicness making his bottom teeth tingle almost sexually, he lets himself again be lulled all over by the curling wall of memory, the wave of mantric propeller dronings . . .

The dream has resurfaced. Not of the war, like you might expect. But all the way back to those earliest memories, earliest inklings. Not since childhood, but every few nights now, though each time with minor revisions and variations. But always as the mutant recollection unspools, a passenger jet approaches overhead with monstrous leisure. Always he is surprised an aircraft that colossal can move so slowly yet remain airborne. Then something sounds wrong. Above him it drifts past, awesome, a titanic beast —

"This will be fun."

Ghady's words snap him back, make him smile. She does like to have fun. Can get fun out of just about any activity. He glances over at his wife while he drives them toward the bird sanctuary adjacent to the bay.

"Where Gamma an' Gamper?" shrills Laila from the safety childseat in back.

"Behind us, see?" Ghady points to the Lincoln following them down the road. Laila squirms and twists to see.

He smiles in the rearview mirror, surprised all over again at how her three year old's enthusiasm for being simply alive sparks him.

His stomach goes queasy then at the thought of tonight. Wait until Laila's in bed asleep. All fun will then cease. Ghady doesn't know. Technically, she hasn't done anything wrong. He wonders if he will have to enumerate the litany of his discontents, which will then, as mere words, make him sound petty and mean spirited. Anyway, how does he know that *any* woman he might ever live with—Muslim, Christian, Jewish, *Druid*, whatever—won't also interrupt his writing, wanting more attention than he has time for? Won't leave him child duties always when the kid's in the worst mood? Won't obsess about money? Won't complain about the-car-the-house-the-life they should but don't have, the spirituality he lacks? Won't sink into tarry moods that make her lash and rip at his own insecurities? Won't undermine his own diminishing hopes that some day he will write the Great American Novel he has planned, always planned, since undergrad days?

"This will be fun," she says, never suspecting.

"You said that."

"But you are now supposed to agree." She giggles.

Her laugh has always been one of her best features. Even now it delights him into laughing in spite of himself. She laughs with an accent.

"I should be working on my dissertation."

"I think the world might continue a few hours longer without 'Celtic and Texan Folklore Sources Used By Robert E. Howard.'"

"That's just the working title."

"Honey, you worked hard all day."

"I stared at the computer all day," he says. He remembers only the clatter of wife, the screeching child banging . . .

"Well, now is for living and enjoying."

"Dah, birdees!"

The toddler bounces, *their* daughter, straining against her kid carseat in back, pointing a cherubic finger out the window at the white dots bobbing high above the water in the dusky sunlight.

"You are so right, Laila," he says.

The words come out in a voice more childish than he likes. Personally he hates that baby-talk tone of voice. But sometimes it comes out anyway.

Look at Ghady objectively, try to simply notice her all over again, without the baggage of the past few years. The top of her head comes only to your chest. The pixie mouth of her olive complexioned, moon face smiles readily; trouble in her brow can still put the squeeze on your heart. Her dark, straight hair has grown past her shoulders again, cut across in Cleopatra bangs. A stranger might glance at her blouse and judge her flat chested, but you know that when you unbutton the material, her bare breasts shaped like ripe yellow mangos turn slightly outward, a nice handful, small, fitting her slight build so you lift her in your arms without strain, her nipples the color reddish peaches have when you take a bite out of them, shading more toward plum as you lick and nibble them, matching the hue of her lower, inside—if memory serves.

He glances in the rearview at his dad tailgating him, now dropping back, then accelerating too fast again, scaring his mother, compensating for gradual physical decline.

Ghady has fun all right, Brad thinks. She has a sense of humor all right. Well developed. Almost as well developed as her Islamic superego. Yeah, Ghadeer al Kame is a regular Madonna, double entendre intended. Westernized enough to have taken his hand that night in Austin four years ago on the south mall of the University and guided his fingers to

THE EXTINCTION OF RHINOS IN MEXICO

feel she was wearing no panties. On the damp cool cushion of ivy and leaves outside Parlin Hall, at the foot of a statue of some Confederate, Brad could just make out, up past Ghady's naked, posting shoulders, Eagle Scout Chuck Whitman's perch, there through the branches of the broad, thickbarked live oak trees. The Tower had been lit up orange that night she took him, heralding some victory.

A few weeks later when she had told him, shyly, a slipped diaphragm, or one too old, he had felt giddy again, like that feral night, stupidly proud, like he was the first one in the world. He thought it was an Islamic thing, her not wanting to get an abortion. She got mad when he said that and told him he didn't know anything about it—Islam or her or abortion. She had him there.

In the face of her withering indictment, shamed at his callous pettiness, he broke down crying and begged her forgiveness. She held him and stroked his hair and murmured her proposal. He had said yes gratefully.

When the plane comes, floating, it casually turns belly up, simply rolls over midair. Dread balloons in his stomach like the bloat of noxious gases within a corpse—he's helpless, with no means of preventing the carnage. The big flying machine yaws over and drops like a slaughtered ox to the tarmac, detonating on impact. An agony of flame roils out. All those dead disgorged, all those charred corpses draped smoldering over buildings and the infinite fence like a Dali painting commissioned by Goya. Dead people all over. As far as the eye can see. Apparently without number. Ashes to ashes, fragments of meat.

This was progress: Death as a plane instead of Freud's locomotive.

Since the invasion he and his wife have taken to watching Peter Jennings and later Ted Koppel each night. Maybe that's why the dream has come back. Previously Ghady always hated news programs for their diet of pap and murder.

Of course, she doesn't exactly cherish them now, watching the jingo parade of weaponry destined for the Middle East: Mavericks, Patriots, Daisy Cutters. Neat names for incontinent butchery.

Shouldn't he leap up from his La-Z-Boy to... do something? He does nothing. Dread presses down on him in his livingroom like the gravity of Jupiter. Vigor mortis.

Some months into their pregnancy, and marriage, they had been in this same vehicle, driving along the brain flattening, featureless stretch of I-37 between San Antonio to Corpus Christi, air conditioner kaput, mercury at 101, the requisite trip to satisfy the usual suspects (the grandparents-to-be—the American set). Ghady made him stop at a Conoco because she had to pee (again!) couldn't wait any longer, bloated with child. She had ambled inside, absolutely unexotic anymore. He gazed at the old service station sign and a nostalgia from childhood had overcome him: *Conoco, Hottest Brand Going!*

Going. While she was inside, he had put the car in gear. That was all.

He knew he wasn't going anywhere. The car was only *called* a Horizon; it was never intended to take him there. It rolled to his job, the university, the Utotem and no place like home. Maybe he didn't exactly love her, but he couldn't do that to her. Not back then.

She's not a horrible person. He would never dream of claiming that. It's just that he should never have married her. It was his mistake. Just too many personality glitches left over now that sex has settled into being just one more (sporadic) item on their neverending list of Things To Do.

He doesn't have all the details worked out, but just committing himself to it in his own head has been liberating. All that afternoon before they left the house, he found he had more energy, was accomplishing more, despite occasional twinges of guilt or nagging affection and tenderness. Even the words of the dissertation began flowing from his brain to the keyboard. Yes, details remain, but sometimes it's better to take the plunge rather than ease in. A clean break. He feels ninety percent certain he can get the court to grant him, the father, (a born U.S. citizen, nominally Christian), custody of Laila over the mother (naturalized Iraqi-American, Muslim). Especially if he injects current politics into the deal.

You shit head.

He pulls into the suburban wildlife refuge, a stone's throw from Corpus Christi Bay. Here along the Cayo del Oso—Bear Shoals—you can spot birds rarely seen anywhere else in the world. Only last April, on a plane from Houston, Brad met a gentleman from Yokosuka, Japan who spent his life-savings to travel all the way across the world to right here to birdwatch. *Tonight I do it. I get it over with.*

"I am so pleased with your earring," says Ghady, caressing his ear near the new tiny diamond stud as he turns off the car.

"Just call me Joe Pirate," he says.

"Do you hate it?"

"No I don't hate it."

"You are horrible."

"I said I didn't hate it."

"You didn't have to get it done if you didn't want to."

"I'm just teasing you."

He makes silly growling noises and nuzzles her. Truthfully, he likes having a pierced ear. Kind of makes up for the Horizon. Things always seem fine so long as he has her in a clinch, and her lips...

"Know what?" he says, Eskimo kissing Ghady, making them both crosseyed.

"What?"

"Sometimes you make me do what I really want to do."

She squeezes his hand.

"Dah's silly!" Laila rejoices.

"Oh, he sure is," he says in the baby voice.

Sometimes that voice is the only one he can manage and still continue. *Forget the lips. Tonight's the night. Hottest brand going.* In the back seat Laila laughs at them.

His parents wheel into the parking lot of the sanctuary in their Lincoln. The father gets out first to help the mother out on her side. He's been doing this for years, even before her arthritis. Despite his liberalism, his manners and attitudes regarding the sexes are Old School.

"Aren't you afraid one of these birds will swoop down and peck that bauble out of your ear?" his father says to him.

"Daddy, I'll risk it. I'm braver than you think."

Both men are grinning. Apes sometimes grin, Brad remembers, a threatening territorial gesture. Gamma chats with Laila and Ghady. He's grateful—and proud, he realizes—that his parents truly like Ghady. Of course, providing his mother with a granddaughter has been a decided boost to international relations. Laila leaps into the thick, still strong arms of Gamper. Brad still isn't used to his parents as grandparents. He wonders how they'll handle his divorce. As long as he gets Laila.

With Laila benched on his arm, Gamper walks with Gamma up the asphalt nature trail that winds through the brush. A brown pelican glides low over the oso, wings brushing ripples in the water. Brad thinks he hears something out of place.

Along the indigenous scrub brush comprising the asphalt nature trail, placards have been constructed revealing the confusion of gnarly, thorny plants to possess distinctions. Mesquite (appellative derived from the Nahuatl); Huisache (genus *Acacia*); Prickly Pear Cactus (*Nopalea cochinillifera*). They seem more significant wearing formal name tags. He had met her and run into her several times before he could get her name straight. He could tell she liked him. When she had no name, she was just another one of those foreign students at

THE EXTINCTION OF RHINOS IN MEXICO

the university. Foreign looking. Then Suzy Bates had dumped him. Ghadeer al Kame. Ghady.

"Pelicans are a primitive type of bird," he starts explaining to Ghady. "Prehistoric." Having passed sentence on their marriage, he discovers he's relaxing with her again. He feels his sad resentments already fading with the expiring sun, the strange sensation that this is a year after tonight, and they're getting together for one of their sporadic family outings, comfortable with their new, separate lives. He now fondly recollects so many morning-after breakfasts with her: piping hot tea, scrambled eggs, salted and heavy on the black pepper, with lemon squeezed over them, brie and Calamata olives with fresh, still warm French bread, and plain creamy yogurt with green grapes. She sits on his lap after they eat, arousing him, smooching with him as she plans his day, a schedule which is thrown hopelessly out of whack when he takes her clothes off again...

"Something to do with that throat pouch," he finishes about the pelicans.

Facing into the warm offshore breeze, Ghady nods and closes her olive-hued eyes.

"My parents will not come."

"Well, we can't make them."

"I think not."

Ahead he watches his own parents disappear with Laila around a corner, into the marsh grasses. He's never met hers, but there have been albums full of photographs and joyous, generous packages across continents and oceans. Once they included some Iraqi beer, and three bottles of the fine, light Scheherezade label made it unbroken. Though her folks grew up when Baghdad had only one paved street, they were educated in London, and now live in a Baghdad congested with Mercedes and Volvos. In the pictures they wear Armani and Christian Dior. Her father has an impish gleam in his dark eyes, and Brad recognizes the mother's dignity in the daughter's face. On the phone they have British accents.

Suddenly Laila comes barreling back down along the path, pumping those stubby little legs as fast as she can go. She reaches them, her mommy and daddy—still odd and curiously wonderful to realize himself as "Dah"—she tags them, then heads back at Gamma and Gamper lickety split.

Ghadeer stops walking and watches her galloping daughter vanishing down that path into the tall cattails, emerging on the far side with her paternal grandparents at the boardwalk. Stilt pilings carry the pier out over the marsh without much disturbing it. The communion of seers out there is festooned with binoculars and cameras. One man peers through a long cannon of a lens set on a unipod, scoping pelicans and egrets. The water and air teem with feeding and settling birds. Seagulls scream in a holding pattern around the pelicans, lurking to divebomb, stealing a fish or two. Old Man Heron pokes about in the shallows for something tasty to spear and eat. A waddle of ducks paddles up a tributary through the grasses and there the birds bob and dive for dinner. In the pinkish orange twilight of this vesper feeding, the humans are contemplative, speaking quietly, if at all.

"Ghady, all we can do is let them know they're welcome here."

"Are they?"

"In our home anyway," he insists, "And at my folks'. You know that."

"Yes, my darling. I don't understand them, my folks."

He says "I guess they figure it's their home and they don't want to abandon it."

"What good is a home if you're buried alive in it?"

Though he sees the tears in her eyes, her voice grates, shrill when she's agitated like this. Gulls swoop down, aggressive panhandlers scolding tourists out of their last breadcrumbs. Something sounds wrong. Wall to wall birds,

THE EXTINCTION OF RHINOS IN MEXICO

he muses. Hitchcock strolls out along the boardwalk for his cameo.

Here comes Laila again, excitement exhaled with her every hurried breath. Tag. There she goes again, precariously balanced on churning sausage legs, our blood mingled in those strong little legs.

He hears them before he sees them. A wall of sound. Across the sky, lumbering in over the bay, the behemoths on parade, one following one following another on and on, the C-5 Galaxy engines sounding like the approaching scream of a million falling angels. Tonnage floating past in slowmo. With monstrous leisure the gargantuans land at the Naval Air Station on the far side of the oso, to refuel and stock up and then take off with their cargo bound for the desert, for Baghdad.

Her pixie cornsilk hair flying, Laila races toward them, her olive eyes wide and bright with the raw joy of moving fast, her face dark complexioned like Ghady, flushed with pure life. Their daughter was born without a name. They hadn't been able to agree until she was three days old, and then another couple of days to negotiate the spelling.

The girl stumbles, upends skidding on her hands and knees. He feels his own skin crawl, his toes curl, yet she looks so absolutely startled *this* could happen that he finds he can't help smiling. On the tarmac she examines her chubby bloodying knee. The gulls flock round, taunting like winged hyenas. She begins crying as Ghady reaches her first. He watches them gathering out over the sea.

Thanks to Technical Ted Koppel, Brad and the whole nation are fully aware of the cargo the planes carry in their bowels. But Ted is a lot of words. He doesn't give the full story, doesn't show what happens when each and every plane is a general store and emporium of canned megadeath.

You got your Multiple Launch Rocket Systems for pulverizing bones, complete with submunitions for splattering brains; you got your basic cluster bombs just right for gooshing hearts and shredding penises; don't forget good old-fashioned bullets for piercing ears, eyes, nose, and throat; and how could we leave out the best fuel-air explosives U.S. dollars can buy for atomizing muscle tissue—into mist, by God (and for God, not Allah)—not to mention glorified Glad Bags for holding liquidy intestines oozing dead stinking shit. On second thought, forget we mentioned the casual ties at all, unless you mean the ragheads and then the more the better, can't trust any of them, not even the damned children for Christ's sake. Learned that in Nam. Better yet, you're not to mention bags or body parts. Just arms. Arms and victory, ladies and gentlemen. Just the Yankee Doodle Dandy soundbite clips we decide to declassify. Jobs and glory and petroleum for America, televised primetime forever and ever, Amen.

New Babylon seeking to destroy Old Babylon.

His daughter runs to the solace of his arms. He kneels beside her. He's startled all over again every time by how alive she is.

"Hey, Lolly Laila. Bet that hurts, huh?" he says in his pal voice. She nods and goes right on bawling, leaning her compact, dense weight against his chest as he examines the damage. He can feel his heart beating against her. Her knee is a little tattered there and bleeding.

"But you're going to have a classic scab. All the kids will want to see it," he says. "It'll all be worth it." That's what they tell us. He blows his fatherly breath over the wound and notices the tiny gravels in the skin they'll have to clean out later and daub with mercurochrome. Monkey blood, Laila likes to call it. How easily the skin tears. She cries and cries.

"Bleeding," she tells mama.

"It's okay, lamb," says Ghady. "It's just a bo bo." She kisses the tears on the girl's cheeks. Laila loves her mother, depends on her mother.

"Is she all right?" his mother asks, coming back, to his eyes still not looking like a grandmother at all.

THE EXTINCTION OF RHINOS IN MEXICO

"It's not so bad," says Ghady.

"Man alive, look at all them," Gamper says, pointing overhead, amazed. The flying hyenas scream. The little girl is all tears. Inconsolable.

"There, there," Brad says, hugging his daughter to him, and then finally his wife as well, for better or worse after all. Together they watch the death shrieking sky. Plane after plane. Apparently they are without number.

8

PAGAR POR SUSTOS

Pagar por sustos. [*El Salvador.*] To buy on credit. [colloq.] Lit. "to pay for frights;" "to pay by fears."

"Agua, 'Paro!"

She could never resist his angel face even when he was grumpy. She worked hard to pronounce his name, but sometimes it still came out as Shuck. She got him a plastic tumbler of water and finally got him down for a nap, reading him the storybook he picked out. No matter what the book, he liked her made up Spanish version better than the real story. He was only just four but his room had as many books and toys as a store. And all the videos, too: *Barney, Thomas the Tank Engine,* and *Wallace and Grommit,* and *There Goes a Monster Truck!* and *There Goes A Rocket!* and every thing from Disney. There were so many. Still, Amparo couldn't resist buying him even more toys, so that he would have things from her. Often she would buy him some toy train he didn't have yet. Chuck never got tired of trains and he loved candy and he loved Amparo. She loved the bright, sunhaired little boy as much as if he was her own. When she would come to work in the mornings Chuck would shriek joyfully: "'Paro's home!" Sure, he was naughty sometimes but only in natural little boy ways that made her laugh when she told her friends Conchita and Alba about it later. Perhaps she loved him more since the

THE EXTINCTION OF RHINOS IN MEXICO

belief began creeping up on her that she might never find a husband.

At the end of the story she closed the book and closed the blinds and kissed him on the forehead, and then she closed the door. He liked the ritual. She had to do it in the same order or he would get mad.

Just before she closed his door he spoke up softly.

"'Paro, we saw a wreck, didn't we?"

"An accident."

"A bad wreck?"

"Sí, Chico."

"What about those ladies?"

"I don't know, Baby."

"They got hurt?"

"Well, they took them to the hospital. "

"That's where they fix people?"

"Yes."

"Did they fix the ladies?"

"Sometimes that takes a long time."

"What would happen if the truck ran into the 'nosserus instead of the ladies?"

"Close your eyes. Go to sleep." She shut the door. *Puchica, what a day.*

You're too American, Conchita always told her. Conchita said that it was one thing to speak your mind when you were just with the girls. *There's plenty of time for giving him your opinions after the priest ties the knot and he doesn't have a choice.*

Plenty of time. What about time for herself? She worked six days a week and didn't get home until eight most nights and then there was the studying for citizenship and reading her bible lessons, which truth be known, she skimped on far too often. Where were the hours for her to meet nice men, much less get to know them in the proper way?

One day while Amparo was still a girl and the war had just started happening, her mother passed by a neighbor's and heard *the small children inside crying. It was a sad house because the mother had already disappeared and the father, who drank too much before, drank even more after his wife was gone. Some said she had been taken by the rich people's death squads and gang raped, then hacked to death with machetes like so many others. Others swore that she had gone north, to San Diego, California. Amparo's mother could not find the father, so she brought the three children to her own home, and although they could not afford it, Tata agreed to it for as long as it took to get one of the government agencies to look after them. One of the children was a cute little boy named Carlos.*

Later, after the agency took the children, Amparo would see Carlos sometimes on her way to school. She would smile and they would chat. Well, she always did most of the talking. Although he was then only a few years older than Chuck was now, Carlos was quiet and diligent. He had already started working at a meatpacking plant. She liked to tease him because he was always serious and polite.

Amparo was tired. She needed to catch some sleep herself, but now found she could not lose herself that way. Not after what had happened. Okay, she would keep busy. She was hired only as a nanny, but she wound up cooking and cleaning and doing laundry just because she liked this family and couldn't stand it if things needed doing and didn't get done because that Tom Harrigan worked all the time and never did a damn thing around the house anyway and Chuck's mother Sarah was gone at her business until seven every night.

Still, Amparo felt very fortunate as she sorted whites from colors and started another load of laundry. Chuck's father Tom produced a top rated sitcom for ABC and his mother Sarah had her own movie prop shop that she had started eight years before with a partner. Sarah was almost like a friend. She would always trade information with Amparo about various actors. Her company had provided props for several of Arnold Schwarzenegger's movies. He was another good one. Sarah

THE EXTINCTION OF RHINOS IN MEXICO

was making him a special prop one time and when she had to stretch the measuring tape all the way around his big chest his muscles were so big that she just had to tease him, so she stopped and said *I have a problem with that.* Arnold took a puff of his cigar and smiled. *Deal with it,* he said back to her, and shared a laugh with Sarah. That's the way she was. Sarah could have had all these autographed photos of stars, but she didn't care about that type of thing. She came from a farm outside of Lawrence, Kansas. Amparo liked working for Sarah because she was generous, down to earth and liked to hear all the dirt from the "Nanny Network." Of course the nanny network was not a true organization. It was just that the nannies who worked for movie people knew each other, and many of these women were from El Salvador, many of them illegals, like Alba. They worked for some of the most famous actors in the world and a lot of more powerful people who nobody outside of Hollywood ever heard of.

The most important thing Sarah Harrigan ever did for Amparo was to sponsor her green card petition. But the nicest thing Sarah ever did was when she cosigned on the papers so that Amparo could buy a completely new Toyota Celica by paying each month "an installment." This way Amparo was also establishing credit. To be in Los Angeles without credit was something many people did, yet Amparo was sharp, she listened and watched the way yanquis did things and realized that no credit meant you would probably not rise very far here. The stupid thing was that you had to have money to get credit. But if you had money you didn't *need* the credit!

Amparo made a mental note to buy more detergent as she crammed the very last dish possible into the dishwasher and emptied the squeeze bottle into the door compartment and then shut the machine and started it. At first she meant to just pay cash for a cheap dependable used car, but Chuck's mother convinced her that she deserved something nice, and that it would be safer for when she drove Chuck around. This car was nothing compared to the Mazarattis or Jaguars or huge Lincoln Navigators racing along Wilshire or Century Park East, but it was nice, very nice for Amparo. She liked to be inside her shiny metallic green Toyota Celica, to smell the new smell of her tan vinyl upholstery. Even when Chuck spilled something or couldn't wait and peed, it wiped right off. You could wash it and it didn't smell bad, but it had stopped smelling new and lately smelled like soap and crackers. But that was all right. The Toyota made her feel like things were good. With this car it was just like one of the tv commercials said: she had freedom. She could take Chuck to any park or store. She could decide to go anywhere and get in and just go there. And when people saw her car, they had respect for her because they saw she had a new, nice car. Credit was one thing, but to be in this city without a car was to be a cripple. Sure there were the buses, but not enough, so that often you had to wait a long time and sometimes the buses were full and would pass you by, and even when you did get on one you had to crowd in and stand the whole way. When did any Anglos ever take a bus? Only the ones who had to, the poor ones. Except for that one tv star who was a fanatic about the environment, and even he quit riding once an electric car came on the market that he could lease for $500 a month. Puchica! No, unless you had a car, and a decent one, you were nobody. She had learned that lesson quickly in the United States.

The season Amparo turned fifteen years old a flood swept through her village. People who had survived years of war died in the flood. It made you wonder. The river washed through her family's house. Her father had been at the newspaper working so her mother rescued Amparo's grandmother, who wouldn't let go of the television. Fortunately their house was built of cinderblocks and was sturdy.

One morning soon after, when the mud was still a foot thick in the house and there was a dirty water mark chest high on the walls and the muck had begun to smell like rotten eggs, which was better than the ripe corpses that still sped by in the river, Amparo and her sister and brothers had been almost ready to walk to school. All the schoolchildren had to wear uniforms, even though it was a state sponsored and not a Catholic school. She hated that uniform and had been arguing with her mother about having to wear it. They were ugly and scratchy and now smelled of mildew even though her mother had washed them. Mami was scolding her when the soldiers came into the house with their guns and smashed the tv and pulled Tata and Mami and her sister Graciela and brothers Tito and Nando and her and even Abuelita out of the house and shoved them all down to the swollen river. Her mother was crying. Her grandmother didn't understand what was happening. The soldiers yelled at her father and slapped him. They hated his small newspaper. Amparo watched a dead cow floating past on its side in the rapid current, seeming to dribble a flat football that had become trapped in the eddies of its stiff front legs. Tata was scared but brave and proud when they pointed their guns at him. Even when they pointed guns at Amparo and the rest of her family. Amparo was shivering because she didn't yet understand this was just a warning, and believing she was about to have her brains blown out, she prayed for Carlos to be well and to remember her sometimes. But a part of her inside was laughing to recall the look on the soldiers' faces when floodwater gushed out of the tv they smashed.

Amparo remembered something else she needed to do. Once a year, Sarah would decide to clean out her and Tom's closets and get rid of a lot of clothes, and she would let Amparo have her pick and then phone Goodwill to take the rest. Amparo now picked through the stacks Sarah had made in the master bedroom. Perfectly good clothes. But these people always bought more, even when they already had plenty. It was just something to do. Amparo chose what she wanted and put them in boxes. Tomorrow she would ship the clothes to her brothers and sister or other family members to wear, give away or sell.

For now, Amparo lay down again and tried to sleep.

The monthly cost of the Toyota was a lot of money for her, and it was hard to have the money every month for when the note was due since she was always wiring part of her paycheck back to El Salvador to help her sister go to the university and for her family to bribe the guards so her father would not be maltreated. Because of the money Amparo sent, he at least had all the bare necessities in the prison and sometimes a comfort or two, and Amparo had never ever missed a car payment until this month but now she was late because the guards had demanded more money. Already she had to buy gasoline and some groceries with her Texaco credit card. She needed to talk to Chuck's mother about the car payment before the bank did.

Gradually Amparo started to drift off in the warmth of the California afternoon with the cool Pacific breeze caressing her and in her ears the pleasant whirrings of the washing machine, the dryer and the dishwasher and the slightly distant sounds of traffic and helicopters. Then, just as she fell asleep there was a screech of tires outside and though there was no thump at the end, she dreamed a thump and she saw again the two old ladies fly strangely through the air and tumble on the hard street.

Amparo awoke with a start.

When Alba answered the phone from the house where she was working that day, Amparo told her about how she had taken Chuck to the zoo for the first time and he was crazy about the rhinoceros he saw, such a strange creature, and couldn't stop talking about it even later at the pony ride in Los Feliz down near I-5. Amparo now pronounced it "Feeless." Nobody in L.A. would know where you were talking about it you said it right. She meant to come right out and tell Alba about the accident first thing, but instead she told Alba how Chuck had been riding the pony, nearly slipping off the saddle, and she saw a man there wearing sunglasses and watching his own son riding a pony. He seemed like a man who really liked seeing his little boy have fun. Later when Amparo was getting Chuck down off his pony, the man was doing the same with his boy. Amparo had to say something.

"You know, you look a lot like John Travolta."

"That's because I *am* John Travolta."

"No!" she shook her head and hid her grin with her hand.

"Really, I am."

"You are just kidding me."

"No, I promise." He took off his sunglasses and smiled so she could see it really truly was John Travolta. He was so normal and without attitude that she had not believed it at first. Alba was gratifyingly impressed and she and Amparo began discussing the merits of various celebrities. Jessica Lange was another one who was regular. Once Amparo was helping a friend at a house where Jessica was a guest, and Jessica rolled up her sleeves and washed dishes right there with them. Oh, but there were some bitches Amparo could tell about. Like that one today. But Amparo also told about the good ones. That's why she had to tell her friend Alba about John Travolta. Though Amparo didn't believe in gossiping, she did believe in letting her other friends who were nannies know what potential employers were like. It was necessary. You never knew who you might end up working for. Over the years Amparo had avoided several bad employers who when they interviewed her treated her so nice, but afterwards she asked her friends and the others and they would tell her how those people really were. Amparo liked where she was now, five days a week with Chuck, babysitting other kids some nights and on weekends.

John Travolta. What a gentleman. And then to have Jack see such a thing. She thought he had been too short in his car seat to be able to catch sight of the broken figures. How much had he seen?. Hardly anything, she prayed. Well, she had seen plenty when she was growing up hadn't she and it didn't ruin her. This was nothing. Yet Amparo realized she wasn't ready to tell Alba about the dead women. Later, not quite yet. It still made her shake to think about it. As Amparo had been driving Chuck home from the pony ride, back to the Miracle Mile district, she went along Los Feliz to where it bends around past Griffith Park and turns into Western and she drove down the hill there with Chuck chattering about the rhinoceros and pretending like a plastic train he had was a rhino and was smashing it into Buzz Lightyear and Amparo turned right on Hollywood Boulevard, the older, rundown stretch with vacant buildings, a porn shop, an Armenian boxing club and on down a row of Thai restaurants. At the crosswalk in front of this dilapidated hotel there was no stoplight so you had to watch out. And sure enough, Amparo had to brake for two strolling elderly women who stepped out into the street without even looking, their arms linked. In her rearview mirror, Amparo glimpsed the Mercedes SUV impatiently swerve, the woman driver on her cell phone. Before Amparo could think, the Mercedes accelerated past her and plowed into the two old women.

Afterwards, the beautiful blonde woman in the big Mercedes kept talking on her cell phone. Her face never changed. Or maybe she looked a little more anxious? ¿Que quiere decir—"Put out?" It was hard to tell; the sunglasses hid the woman's eyes. But her attitude was what made Amparo shake more than anything else.

Neighborhood people came running out and a man began screaming. Vagrants and other lost ones watched as some good samaritans knelt beside the women lying twisted and broken on the potholed street.

"What happened, Amparo?" Chuck had asked. He was straining, trying to see. Fortunately, he was too short to see much. But enough. "Was that noise the ladies?"

THE EXTINCTION OF RHINOS IN MEXICO

"An accident, Baby. That's all."

When the police arrived, they couldn't get the woman to come out of the big Mercedes. In fact, she tried to drive off and the angry police had to run their car in front of her to stop her. Both cars were on the wrong side of the street then, in front of a place strangely named St. Andrew's Liquor. It caused a big traffic jam.

They let Amparo stay close to Chuck in the Toyota while she told them exactly what she had seen. The police thanked her and took her phone number and let her take Chuck home. A tv news van had arrived and a couple of helicopters hovered loud overhead. A pretty lady ran over with a cameraman and they wanted to ask Amparo questions. She could have been on tv, but she didn't want Chuck to see any more, so she drove away and the lady interviewed one of the derelicts. Amparo guessed it would be on the Channel 9 news that night.

All the way home Amparo had thought about the women and scarcely heard Chuck prattling. They looked foreign to her. Perhaps Russian. Probably Armenian. What a thing to come to a new country and die like that.

He worked hard for years and saved his money and grew to be a tall, handsome youth. Shy as he was, one day Carlos stole a kiss from Amparo. She didn't mind. They secretly kissed many times after that, his tongue intertwining with hers until her knees couldn't hold her up. She couldn't even confess this to the priest. Even though she was five years older, Carlito solemnly vowed that he was going to marry her when he was a man.

Yet before he could do anything else, he told Amparo, he had to find his mother if she was alive. He journeyed by himself to the United States, to San Diego. He was gone so long, but Amparo waited.

Before Amparo became Chuck's nanny, one very famous couple had invited Amparo to interview about being their nanny—one of several. This couple had adopted five children and were going to get a nanny for each one. The young actor and his wife were both very beautiful and Amparo liked them and listened to all they had to say, but in the end she had to tell them No because they were forthright and explained to her that the marriage was simply for the public appearance. The actor was a maricón, and here in Hollywood that was nothing, but as a matter of business, it had to be kept secret from the outside world. Some of the nannies felt that the secret was so that the women who adored him would not be disappointed, but Sarah and Amparo talked it over and decided that the secret was really for fans who were men. The secret was so important that when one of those trashy tabloids that everybody likes to look at in the grocery found out and wrote about it, the couple took them to court. It didn't matter that in this case the tabloid had mostly told the truth. The couple had the most expensive lawyers, so in the end the court made the periodical print a retraction saying No it wasn't true what they printed about the actor being a maricón. Amparo believed that the young actor truly cared for his wife. No one knew for sure, but it was said the actress got paid a certain amount and probably got a movie role and for two years she was not allowed to see any other men, but after that, her contract let her, but only if no one found out about it. Amparo had a good reputation, that's why the couple asked for her, but she had to tell them No, because what they were doing was a sin. In reality, she liked them both, and personally, she didn't care, but the Church said it was an abomination in the eyes of God.

After the war she was still in school when a friend of her father escorted her on a trip to market, a man from the neighborhood who wore a thick gold chain, although the water didn't always run through the pipes of his house. This Señor _____ was very pious, always in church or at home reading the Bible. She didn't ask him to escort her, but there he was, walking respectfully a little ways behind her. When she stopped to see the new dress in the window of Fashions Mimi, he also stopped. Sometimes she stopped for no reason at all, just for the fun of

THE EXTINCTION OF RHINOS IN MEXICO

making him stop as well. At the market she paused in the entrance by the pupusería, and looked back. Señor _____ paused, just as if he and she were linked and she smiled at him, he always seemed like a gentleman just tonguetied and she had decided to go talk with him when out of nowhere a guy rushed at him, snatched the gold chain and raced down the street. Very quickly Señor _____ pulled out a 9mm pistol and fired five or six times. The thief fell. It happened like an ordinary event so that it was over before she knew it.

Señor _____ went and stood over the guy and crossed himself. When he came back over to her he said We'll have to split up. This type are often in the hire of the police.

With that he left her. Amparo decided the crowded market would be just as good a place as any, but before she even had time to mix into the crowd, she heard tires squeal. Turning, she saw Señor _____ at the wheel of a car, speeding away up the street. Where did the car come from? Did he have it parked there all along, ready for a lightning getaway? Or did he steal it? Curious now, she wandered over to where the thief lay twitching on a spreading pool of viscous crimson and urine. In his hand Amparo could see the gold chain, clutched tightly as if he meant to take it with him to wherever he was going now. She never found out why Señor _____ did not take back his chain, but the next time she saw him, he had a gold chain around his neck. She often wondered if it was the same one.

The phone was ringing when Sarah got home and Amparo had her arms full of laundry. Sarah came grinning to Amparo with the portable. She smiled a lot and that was another reason Amparo liked working for her.

"It's for you."

"Who is it?" Amparo whispered, dropping the hot clean clothes on the couch to fold. She was suspicious of the mischief in Sarah's eyes.

"They didn't say, but I think it's your fan club."

Amparo took the phone and as Sarah left Amparo recalled she needed to ask her for an advance so she could pay the car payment. On the phone it was the Warner children. Often at night after Sarah got home, Amparo would go babysit the Warner children for an hour or so and sometimes all day on Saturday. Each of the three was on a different phone.

"Why did you quit?"

"I didn't quit."

"Mommy says you're not coming anymore."

"That you quit."

"I didn't quit."

"Then you'll come over tomorrow?"

"No. How is your arm Shawna?"

"It has a grody scab," said Jimmy.

"It does not," Erin said.

"At least she was brave enough to climb the tree," said Amparo.

There was this little scrape on the inside of Shawna's upper arm where she tried to hug the tree when she slipped and fell. Scarcely any bleeding. No broken bones. Just a lot of crying. You would have thought it was the end of the world to hear Mrs. Warner tell it. But what was the use of a beautiful, manicured yard if you never used it?

"When are you coming over, 'Paro?"

"Baby, I'm not no more. Allí no mas. Maybe I'll still see you sometime at the park."

"When?"

"We'll see."

"Por favor, 'Paro."

"Por favor! Por favor!"

"We'll be good and not let Shawna climb any trees."

"And maybe Jimmy won't wet his pants anymore."

"Shut up! I'll make Erin and Shawna clean up the whole every bit of the house for you, 'Paro."

"I don't think so, pee pee boy." Erin and Shawna giggled.

"'Paro!" He started crying.

"Hush you brats."

"It's your fault Shawna. You don't ever mind."

"Zip it. Chico, I don't care if your sister climbs. Or if any of you does. You're kids, that's what it's about. You just got to be a little careful."

"Then why are you leaving?"

"Don't worry about it. I'm not going anywhere. I'll be around."

"Here?"

"No, Baby." She was going to miss these devils after all.

"Pretty please?"

"No."

"Mommy says you quit because you don't like us."

"She said that?" *Puchica, that lady.* "Look, I still love you Erin. And Jimmy and Shawna too, understand? You want to know why I'm not coming anymore? Because your mother is full of shit."

There was silence on the other end of the line. Then three little giggles.

After a year and a half in the United States, Carlos found his mother. By then she had remarried and had new babies. His mother told Carlos that she had been too young when she got married. That she never had any feeling for him.

By the time Carlos returned to El Salvador, the war had ended and work was hard to find. Anyway he was different by then. He began taking things from people and would beat them if they protested. From the United States he brought back dirty Mexican words, like cholo. *He called himself a cholo, he had seen how gangs operated in the United States and began gathering his own mara of cholos around him. Before long he and his gang were regularly plundering in five towns and villages. People hated him, but they were also afraid. Amparo waited, but he never called on her.*

Amparo drank a lot when she first got to the United States of America. She drank because she was happy and scared and lonely and it helped her to speak English. She gained weight, she knew she was getting too heavy. *All right,* she would admit to herself, *fat. But not soft fat.* Still, in Los Angeles every billboard and every magazine ad, even in the Spanish periodicals showed only *flacas*, bony women who would be lucky if they could carry one kid, let alone two. When she finally got the chance to visit El Salvador again, people looked at her extra weight and nodded *Ah, you're doing well.*

Amparo knew Conchita and Alba from the church she went to. They were Salvadoran, but they spent disgusting amounts of their earnings on liposuction and plastic surgery. Conchita used the same doctor as the lady in Brentwood who lived two blocks from the O.J. house before they tore it down, who hired Conchita to clean her mansion and six toilets.

"You get what you pay for," Conchita whispered to Amparo in English one Sunday, putting twenty dollars in the offering plate. Amparo put five. If that wasn't good enough for God, so be it. One time some repair men even came by the house where Alba was cleaning and mistook her for the owner because she looked so perfect. Amparo had to admit that Alba did look like a movie star now, but she didn't even have a car. Amparo had taken to calling Conchita *Concha* now that the shameless *niña* finally went so far as to have a plastic surgeon make her privates tight again like a virgin. Alba laughed and it made Conchita angry when Amparo called her the dirty slang and they both reminded Amparo that rich, respectable *yanqui* women did it all the time and showed her the large brazen advertisements in the *L.A. Weekly*. All Amparo could say was that she didn't have to pay a doctor.

"Yes," smiled that bitch Concha, "but no man can appreciate it."

Amparo's cheeks burned and her eyes stung. She knew she was shaped like her Mayan ancestors—a wide head and a flat nose with high cheekbones and plain black hair. Her teeth were strong and white and she had breasts like large papayas, with reddish brown nipples above a broad round stomach. Her complexion was naturally and perfectly tanned even with no sun and she was tall, if wide, and her legs were slim

THE EXTINCTION OF RHINOS IN MEXICO

and well toned from all the walking she did with Chuck. She mostly dressed comfortable in running shoes, shorts and a big t-shirt with Warner Bros. or Disney or Universal on it. Whenever Chuck jumped into her arms and laid his head on her shoulder, her heart ached and her insides contracted with yearning.

Her father had agreed with her that he should bring some men. A *few months earlier a woman they knew had been on the verge of leaving El Salvador with several members of her family. They had everything packed up, every last possession. On the road to the airport they were stopped and robbed of everything and an uncle and son were killed. Things did not stay calm for long after the war.*

The heat and the sun when she stepped off the plane weighed on Amparo like a wet wool blanket from an oven. She had gotten spoiled by the coolness of Los Angeles. When Amparo paid the mordida in yanqui dollars to the customs inspectors, she knew that would not be not all. They would alert others.

Amparo saw Tata. With her father came two short, small young indios she had never seen. Bowlegged, with broad faces the color of mahogany. Puchica, *she thought.* So this is Tata's understanding of our danger?

Out front a beige 1970s Buick was waiting. Señor _____ got out to open the trunk. The two scrawny fellows struggled with the luggage and the microwave and the new television for her grandmother. Amparo was certain she could kick both their asses.

Tata drove and Amparo sat in the middle between him and Señor _____. Nobody said much. The little guys in back didn't say anything. Sure enough, a carload of young men drove out of the airport parking lot behind them. The Buick had good air conditioning and Amparo set it all the way on five. There was a rattle in the fan.

As Amparo's father drove them out of town, the sedan with the young men stayed behind them. The sedan was so full it made Amparo think of the clown car she had seen at Ringling Brothers with Chuck.

He had been so little at the time that the noise and commotion made him cry in fear.

Amparo kept looking back. She looked at Señor _____ beside her. He had his gold chain on, but she did not see any 9mm. The two turkeys in the back seat sat like lumps, never giving the car behind them so much as a glance. No one said anything. Amparo noticed that her tata was older, more gray hair than ever, and smaller. It saddened her because it seemed sudden; she had held a picture of him in her mind that was four years behind, like an old magazine. But he had aged three times that.

She knew the lush selva with the afternoon sun cutting through the leaves should be beautiful, the piercing sunlight and dark shadow tattooing over them as the car went winding up the mountain beneath the canopy. She loved the damp leafy musk of the forest and she needed to relish the songs of all the bright colored birds and the lushness after the constant traffic and concrete and smog of Los Angeles, but the cold noisy air conditioner was delightful and anyhow the thick green of the trees and undergrowth had become accomplices of the maras in the other car, hiding their sins. There was no one else on the road but the two vehicles.

Even over the air conditioner she heard the engine of the other car as it surged. She looked and saw the carload of men speed up alongside Tata, windows rolled down. Tata drove steadily and the young men in the car beside him pulled up bandanas over their faces and she could not hear the metal click as they inserted clips into their automatics, only the air conditioner.

In the seat beside Amparo, Señor _____ twisted around and exchanged a glance with the two little men behind her. If there was a signal she did not detect it, but the shrimp on the side closest to the other car rolled down the window. The equatorial air gushed in and all smells of the country and exhaust from the two straining cars. Shrimp Number 2 brought out his rocket launcher from under the Amparo's seat and aimed it out at the other car. The eyes of the masked men widened in fear and their hands waved No No. Their car braked and swerved, skidding off into the barranca and

THE EXTINCTION OF RHINOS IN MEXICO

rolling over. Never even had to shoot the rocket. Amparo and the shrimps watched it all out the back window. She felt a burst of joy and she laughed with the shrimps while Tata drove and Señor _____ read his bible and never looked at the countryside.

One day Sarah asked Amparo if she had a sweetheart. That's all it took. Amparo broke down crying, it couldn't be helped, and Sarah stroked her head and listened while Amparo told how much it had cost her to ship a $1200 used Ford Ranger to El Salvador for her sister Graciela. Just a few years ago it would have been much cheaper, but now all the tariffs had gone up. Still, it was cheaper than buying a truck in El Salvador. Graciela was a doctor in the city hospital, but sometimes she had to drive to the rural villages to help people. Amparo was so proud of her younger sister. For eight years Amparo had been also sending money putting Graciela through university and then medical school. Now Graciela was a doctor and also married to a doctor. But in El Salvador that didn't make you rich. Amparo had wanted to go to college too, but her sister was the smarter one.

"I'll make a deal with you," said Chuck's mother. "You promise to enroll and study hard and get good grades, I'll promise to make it home by six on the nights you have classes. Who knows, you might meet some nice guy in class and kill two birds with one stone. Y'ever think of that?"

I'm already twenty nine, was what Amparo was thinking. *Almost thirty, and there's no one for me.*

For a while after the war the police tried to become civilized and go by the rules on the model of the United States. Yes, for a time after the war, everything was more or less peaceful. But the war had ruined many things and there were not nearly enough jobs. The mara youths would taunt the police, who hated these gangs but were no longer allowed to respond with force like before. And there was a lot of crime. It didn't have to be a gold chain. If you were wearing a baseball cap that somebody liked, they would shoot you for it. Anything. The police began to return to the ways they were used to from the war.

The last time she visited she walked down the street where the maras hung out and whistled and called at women and hassled men and boys. Most people didn't like when they had to go that way. They became scared and hurried along. But Amparo had plenty to eat always and her arms had grown strong from carrying so many children. She stopped and faced their leader, looking him right in the eyes.

"Do I know you?" she asked.

"No, but maybe you'd like to."

"Look, I know Carlito."

"Sure you do."

"He's my novio. Tell him I said 'Hi.'"

She talked to them. She did not mind the give and take. She asked them who they were. They spoke in English, proud that they could. At first they only told her their dirty gang names. She did not accept that and made them tell her their true names and they did. Tauro, Jorge, Faustino, like that. These young men spoke English well. They had been to the United States but had either gotten deported or they came back when they couldn't get work and grew homesick. Now they all wanted to go back north.

"Why don't you get a job here and save money?" she told the one called Slayer but whose real name was Jesús Maria.

"What job do we get? Where? Tell us."

A police car drove by. The police men called to her. "Are you okay, Señora?"

"It's Señorita and yes, I'm fine, thank you."

"Those aren't the type you should talk with."

"We're just having a conversation," one of the maras said.

"I'm talking to the lady, faggot," said the policeman.

"It's okay," Amparo said. The police car did not leave, but slowly cruised down and around the block and came back by several times. Amparo was in reality on her way to visit a friend of her mother's who wanted advice about the United States. Amparo asked

THE EXTINCTION OF RHINOS IN MEXICO

directions from Guillermo, the leader of the gang, who went by the handle "Jackie Chan" because he had once taken some taekwon-do lessons in Los Angeles near Sunset and Western next to that Mexican Pentecostal church. He told her some directions.

"Now is this really the way?" she asked. "Or are you sending me down a blind alley where you'll be lying in wait?"

The youths all laughed because they knew that she knew how they were.

"We would never do that to the novia of Carlito."

It all happened at once, the way things sometimes do in Hollywood when you're already successful. Chuck's father Tom got a two year long first look feature film development deal with some French investors, and the sale of Sarah's prop company went through, meaning that the whole Harrigan family would be living in Provence, which Sarah explained to Amparo was in the south of France. And of course they wanted to take Amparo with them for the two years.

But difficulties cropped up almost immediately. The French authorities balked at the idea of a Central American nanny taking work away from their au pairs. And then there was the whole issue of the her being a resident alien of the United States. Once you had your green card you couldn't leave the U.S. three hundred and sixty five consecutive days without special permission. That was the law. Applications were made, but later for some reason the people at Laguna Niguel couldn't seem to find the application papers of one Amparo Maria Del Pilar, OTM El Sal. They told her she could either wait and hope for the best, or begin the process over again. Even then there were no guarantees she would get permission. And on the far side of the ocean the French immigration office was digging in its heels.

Amparo told Sarah Harrigan she didn't think she would like France anyway, and besides, it was too far away from her own family. Disappointed, Sarah wrote for Amparo a glowing letter of recommendation. Chuck was really too young to understand what was happening, but Amparo thought her heart was going to break like they always talked about in the telenovelas.

At first she wasn't worried at all about getting another position, but the weeks passed and then the Harrigans were ready to fly off to France and Amparo still hadn't found found any fulltime work. Mrs. Warner left messages on her machine, but Amparo never returned the calls. Amparo's friends in the nanny network told her of openings, and Amparo would phone, but it was always too late somehow. Nobody was even calling her in to interview.

The day the Harrigans left for France, Amparo drove them to LAX in her Toyota. They offered to take a shuttle, but Amparo insisted. She'd been preparing herself and Chuck for this time, but he still didn't listen very well. He delighted in seeing all the airplanes, and after they found parking he took her hand and his mommy's hand as they walked across to the terminal.

"Are we going on one those?" he asked disingenuously with big smiling eyes as a jumbo jet lumbered in overhead with a terrific roar.

"Yes, we're going on one of those," said Tom Harrigan. "For a long time. And you're going to sit in your seat and be a good boy, aren't you Chuck?"

Chuck put on his dejected look and appealed to his mother and Amparo.

"Aren't you, Chuck?"

Chuck nodded and looked up at his father. "You're coming too, Daddy?"

"That's right," chuckled Sarah, exchanging a glance with Amparo. "We're all going together."

Tom Harrigan smiled then and grabbed up his son and lugged him under his arm. "Maybe we'll just throw you in with the luggage. Would you like that?"

The little boy giggled. "No! You're squishing me!"

THE EXTINCTION OF RHINOS IN MEXICO

The flight was delayed and then delayed again. Tom Harrigan started fuming and Chuck was whiney. Tom went to the service desk to demand satisfaction.

"I think now would be a good time," said Amparo.

"So do I," said Sarah. She gave Amparo a big hug. "You take care and let us know where you're working."

Amparo nodded. "Send me pictures."

"We will."

Chuck was at the big glass wall, transfixed, gazing out at the jumbo jets. Amparo came over and knelt beside him. He glanced over at her and smiled.

"We're going on that one?"

"Not that one. But one like it. You are."

He scrutinized her. "'Paro, you're crying."

She quickly brought out the small stuffed rhinoceros. Her credit card was refused at Toys R Us, but fortunately she had had enough grocery cash on her. And, well, God was going to have to make do without his five bucks for a couple of weeks.

"Thank you, 'Paro!"

Chuck was delighted with the toy. After a total of about ten seconds he handed it back to Amparo.

"You hold it."

"No, you've got to hang on to it yourself. I'm staying here."

The boy looked at her, worried. "You're leaving?"

"No, you and your mom and dad are going. You're going to live in a new place for a while."

He grabbed her hand and began to pull her over to his mother. "And you're coming too."

"No, Baby. You're going to have to be a big boy, now, okay Chuck?" She said his name carefully and the C H came out correctly. The little boy nodded tearfully.

In the end she had to walk away and as she went back along the terminal corridor she could hear behind her Chuck in his mother's arms bawling "I want Amparo! I want Amparo!"

* * *

About six weeks after Amparo had seen the old women run over, Mrs. Warner called her on a Saturday. Mrs. Warner was going to ask Amparo to come watch the kids the next evening during a big party they were going to have at their house. Amparo already knew this. She had been talking with Arcelia, the regular nanny for the Warners, who had recently quit after ten years. She just got fed up with those people being so cheap and treating her like she was stupid. She knew from the other nannies that no one would take the job because the kids were such devils for most people.

"I'm so glad I caught you, Amparo. I'm in a pickle. I need someone to watch the children during the party tomorrow night."

"Sunday? That's my day off."

"Oh? From what I hear, you have *every* day off now."

Amparo didn't know what to say. She said nothing.

"If it's church you're worried about, I wouldn't need you until six p.m. Look, the kids know you, Amparo, so I thought that perhaps I could convince you to come back and do this for me."

Over the receiver Amparo could hear car horns honking and knew that Mrs. Warner was calling from her cell phone while driving.

"Aren't you afraid I might drop them from the third floor window or something?"

"Don't be snippy. It isn't attractive. I was very concerned that day. What kind of mother would I be if I weren't? Still, perhaps I spoke hastily. The party will be from six until one a.m. Fifty dollars. And if all goes well, then who knows? Oh, and please be here by five forty five."

"Sorry, but I can't do it for less than a hundred and fifty."

Now Mrs. Warner was silent. For a moment.

"That's highway robbery. I never expected you to be so

THE EXTINCTION OF RHINOS IN MEXICO

greedy."

"It's what I always ask for last minute jobs." It wasn't, but Amparo did not want to go. It was true she needed the work. Since the Harrigans left she had found a little babysitting and some housekeeping, though not enough. But this woman! One hundred and fifty dollars wouldn't even buy one blouse at Mrs. Warner's Rodeo Drive dress shop. Her kids weren't even worth one blouse to her? And those designer clothes she had there were sewn by ladies scarcely able to afford food for their children.

"It's ugly to take advantage," said Mrs. Warner.

"Yes it is."

"You think you've got me over a barrel, don't you?"

"Well, it's up to you."

Mrs. Warner hung up. Pretty soon Mr. Warner called back and she liked Mr. Warner all right and reminded him that she had been fired and why would they want her back?

"Amparo, don't let her get to you. You know you do a good job. I know you do. Think of the children. You know that nothing Alexis says about you will be taken seriously by anyone. Be above this."

Amparo couldn't help but laugh. Mr. Warner knew how his wife was.

"I don't think I want to."

"I probably shouldn't say anything," he said carefully. "But you know her circle does stick together. And there are really only about a dozen agencies in Los Angeles. If you catch my drift."

She did not know what for sure he meant by "drift," but a chill raked up Amparo's spine as if somebody had walked on her grave.

"Now you know our kids adore you. Nobody else will deal with them."

"They're good if you know how to handle them," stammered Amparo. She swallowed. She couldn't breathe right or think clearly, could feel rising panic and desperation. "Anyway, like I told Mrs. Warner, tomorrow's my day off."

"How much?"

"She was only going to pay fifty."

"How much do you want?"

"I asked her for a hundred and fifty and she hung up on me."

"Why don't we make it a hundred and sixty for the evening, and then we'll talk longer term."

The next morning Conchita arrived at church mad as a wet hen because she had to take the bus. She waved her cell phone at Amparo. She had tried and tried to call Amparo. Amparo shrugged; she never answered her phone on her day off and turned the volume down on her answering machine.

"What happened to your Mazda?" asked Alba, who had neither a phone nor a car. She used the pay phone at the pulpería or borrowed Amparo's.

"It got repossessed."

"Well, you don't pay your bills." Amparo had no sympathy even though her Texaco card was maxed out and yesterday she had received from the bank a nasty letter threatening to take away her own car if she didn't pay the payment and the penalty by the end of next week. They had not been able to get in touch with the cosigner, Mrs. Harrigan. They warned Amparo that her credit would be ruined.

"I have to borrow some money," Conchita pleaded.

"Don't look at me."

"Please. You have it, I know you do."

"But I don't have it."

"I need it."

"So do I."

Alba said, "Conchita, it's not like before. Pretty soon she's going to be borrowing from you."

"You need to learn to what to spend your money on," Amparo said.

"That's the way you're going to treat me?"

"You had the money, you threw it away. You're not a movie star."

"You know who comes into that house where I work? I've got to look good. I've got to look great."

"Well, one good thing, since you'll be walking more, you won't have to pay for no more liposuction." Mass started and Amparo began repeating over and over to herself *Mr. Warner is nice enough, the kids are not too bad, Mrs. Warner spends most of her day at the dress shop so she won't be around. Amen.*

The priest was saying what he always said.

Amparo thought that maybe next week she might try going to the pentecostal church that another nanny had been bugging her to go to. But she didn't have much faith left. All the churches she had been to just talked about meekness.

That afternoon Amparo bathed a second time and dressed in her best lavender pantsuit and took her time putting on her makeup and she was already outside going to her car when she heard the phone ring inside.

"Son of a —" She caught herself. Better if she didn't succumb to the habit of cursing in English. Still, she had a sense that she should answer the phone this time, so she broke her own rule and unlocked the door and went back inside and her answering machine clicked on. She turned up the volume and then after her own voice she heard her mother.

"Mami, I'm here. Why are you calling? What's wrong?"

"Can't I call my daughter without her thinking something terrible has happened?"

"Sure, Mami." But she knew her mother's voice when she was trying to be brave.

"Well, Carlito is dead."

It was amazing how clear the line connection from El Salvador was.

"I'm afraid it is so," her mother was saying. "Already the

police and army don't like us, and now people say that the maras are blaming our family for Carlito's execution."

"That's ridiculous."

"They think your father had something to do with it."

"But he's in jail!"

"Nevertheless. We need to come up there."

"What?"

"To the United States. With you."

Complications mushroomed in her head. "I don't know if it's possible. And what about Tata?"

"What good will we do him if we ourselves are arrested or murdered? Who knows even if someone might be listening in on this telephone right this very second?"

"Mami, it will take money." *So much money.*

The last time while Amparo was visiting, Señor _____ was disappeared. Tata was elected head of a neighborhood delegation that sought an audience with Carlos and Amparo went with them fearfully. Tata told Carlos to his face that he had to quit treating people so cruelly.

Carlos swore at her father and made the delegation leave. Amparo cried and told Carlos she hated him. The next day it was heard all around the village that Carlos had vowed to kill Tata.

Amparo's mother cried and her father made plans to slip away to another town during the night. But it proved unnecessary. Someone got word to the father of Carlos and the old drunkard sought out his son. They had not spoken for nearly six years.

"Carlito, you cannot do this," the father said. "You cannot kill this man."

"Tell me why not, Borracho."

"I will." He then told Carlos the story about the time the father was off drunk and left the kids by themselves for days, and how Amparo's father and mother took Carlos and his siblings in and fed them. Of course, Carlos knew everything that the old man told him, but it had been long ago and he not remembered it so clearly or with such passion. He heard his father and began to listen and the

THE EXTINCTION OF RHINOS IN MEXICO

vague recollection of his childhood became refreshed and clear. There were tears dripping into the old man's dirty beard by the time he finished. Carlos withdrew the death sentence against Tata and never bothered him or let any of the other maras. But then Tata got arrested by the authorities and his printing press smashed. Even Carlos couldn't stop that from happening.

Nobody wanted to know who gave up Carlos. Everyone was just glad they didn't have to be afraid of him any more. The death squad tortured Carlos for some time and when they finally strangled him with an electrical cord his tongue, they say, stretched out like a fat purple snake down to his chest.

Amparo arrived at five thirty. The Warner house was in Bel Aire. It wasn't even a house, it was like a village. They had a large tract of land and a dozen servants and groundskeepers. They never bought vegetables because they had the gardener grow whatever they wanted. Mr. Warner was not related to the movie studio. Mrs. Warner grew up in Orange County, but Mr. Warner had moved from Cleveland. He had a big plumbing store in Pomona, but Mrs. Warner always liked to let people think that her husband was a relative of the movie studio family. He bought her the dress shop on Rodeo so she would have something to do.

It was going to be a huge party. Guests were already arriving in big shiny new cars that cost more than a house in the valley. There were the usual stretch limousines.

The Warner children caught sight of Amparo and all ran and hugged and pulled on her. "'Paro! 'Paro!"

Mrs. Warner came in. "There you are. I was wondering what happened to you." Behind her came a Guatemalan woman Amparo had met a few times named Delia. Delia wore a white maid uniform Amparo had never seen her in. It had a little hat and all the white material made Delia's brown skin look even darker. The Guatemalan woman stood back and to one side of Mrs. Warner, and greeted Amparo with her eyes. Delia was holding a sack.

"There is one thing I need you to do before I leave you to the children," said Mrs. Warner.

Amparo looked at Delia. Mrs. Warner took the sack and handed it to Amparo.

"Your check's in there as well. One hundred and sixty U.S. dollars."

Amparo looked inside, then crumpled the bag shut and shoved it back at Mrs. Warner. "I'm not no maid."

The doorbell rang. In the distance Amparo could see more guests in tuxedos and furs being greeted at the door by the butler.

"But, dear, you must wear the uniform. It's brand new and makes everything more festive."

Then you wear it, thought Amparo, but she held her tongue.

"This is a special occasion. We're celebrating freedom. The freedom of my dearest friend in the world."

Amparo saw the blonde lady, then, the beautiful driver who had been on her cell phone when she ran down the two Armenian ladies. She came in the big front door with her husband. The butler took her mink stole. She was elegantly slender and without her sunglasses quite lovely. Everyone was congratulating her. She smiled graciously and looked as if she felt a little sheepish.

"I just want to put this behind me," Amparo heard her say. The husband said something that ended with "proves the system does work."

Someone handed the woman a drink.

Amparo let the sack drop on the floor.

Little Jimmy picked it up. "Here, 'Paro. You dropped this."

The children were tugging now on Amparo, "Play with us! Tell us a story!"

Mrs. Warner smiled that smile. "Yes, put on your uniform and tell the children a story. Por favor."

Amparo stood paralyzed. Tears of poison rage stung her eyes. The bank was waiting for their money. Tata's guards

THE EXTINCTION OF RHINOS IN MEXICO

were waiting for their money. Her family was waiting for their money. And Mrs. Warner was demanding the steepest payment of all. Amparo thought of Carlos. *Mi Carlito*. If only she had him with her, Carlito and his machete, she would make everything right. But they had gotten her poor sweetheart and they got the Armenian ladies and now they got her.

Amparo took the sack from the child and opened it.

9

Guardian

In this neighborhood you see a lot of the newly blind with their sunglasses and new sticks like long conductor's wands. They listen carefully to their instructors. They listen more carefully than they ever listened to anyone before in their lives. Because that instructor is telling them how to conduct their lives to keep from getting nailed by a car. Even the blinded do whatever they can to make this dream last longer. Want one of these? It's an Arturo Fuente Curly Head Deluxe. Popular with my grad students. Decent smoke for the price.

No, that's not my bus. I'm not waiting for any bus. I'm just on the bench, enjoying Arturo, watching the traffic scat by like they all've got someplace vital to get to in their rolling metal coffins. Hell, half of them probably rushing to the Utotem. Gotta buy that lottery ticket. Might hit that $20 million jackpot. Might live to be a hundred and twenty five too.

I never play any of those things. Happen to have a revulsion for lotteries in any way, shape or form. See, I got drafted in just about the last lottery of the Vietnam war. When Mark Struzick heard the news, he took himself to the recruiting office and swore his own damn self in. That's the kind of fool best friend I had. Look, I've got an extra cigar if you want one. Suit yourself.

Nobody wanted to be the last to die. *No vale la pena.* Not

THE EXTINCTION OF RHINOS IN MEXICO

worth the pain. No way, *no por nada*. "No wayner," as Mark abbreviated. By the day before Easter, 1972, they'd been shelling us almost nonstop since Wednesday. Blanketing clouds and heavy rains washed out any chance for an air response. Breathing was like drowning, the tropical atmosphere a stew of shit, mildew, burning tires, and a pig's head this sad looking, wrinkled old man was barbecuing for his last supper.

Of course if you smoke cigars you might wind up with your jaw rotted away like Freud or U.S. Grant. But it's always going to be something, isn't it? Name your poison. Nobody lives forever.

You knew it was something seriously bad from the babel of refugees and deserting ARVN flooding south from Quang Tri. Along the way the South Viet conscripts were ditching helmets, web belts, full ammo packs, M-16s, shirts, pants, boots—anything to do with us. Some of these soldiers wore only mud-caked underwear, and rags on their feet.

Oxen, pigs, grandfathers hugging their chickens, mothers suckling their babies, and orphans stopping to play with the jetsam of the deserters—the line stretched to the low, gray southern horizon.

That night we got the intelligence: ten thousand NVA had swarmed across the DMZ into Quang Tri province, and were hauling ass down the French built Highway 1. We didn't need no stinkin' intelligence to know that they were aiming to link up with their comrades, twenty thousand strong already. Not good numbers.

Sometime in the night the shelling ceased. Then came the order: some fuckwad in a bunker office decided we needed to go take a looksee out up the road.

Near dawn we saddled up and along with our own contingent of three ARVN, headed out into the noisy night.

"Search and avoid," said Toño.

"Five by five, Sarge," I acknowledged. That was what I

wanted to hear. That was the key to survival at that late stage of the game.

Two and a half klicks north, our map led us east, off the pocked, jammed highway, away from the refugees who trudged relentlessly, even in darkness, like zombies from *Night of the Living Dead*.

Our map took us through a rice paddy marked as having been cleared. But in country you learn mighty fast that no map shows all the territory, so we were walking on hollow eggs. I was point man, drenched in angry fear. After me a ways back came Mark, Efrem Sondberg from Cleveland, and Bogie Kocerik from Kansas City, MO. Then Toño and the three young South Vietnamese soldiers.

"Motherfucking conejo!"

I whirled my M-16 around at Toño's voice. He and the others were looking back and I was scared they had seen some VC coming at us from behind. But what we saw in the twilight was one of our ARVN privates splashing through the paddy, hightailing it. Pissed as hell, I broke and ran past Mark and the others. I was going to bag that chickenshit.

"MacIntyre, get back here!" Toño shouted at me.

"Ngung! Dó bân con chó nhút nhát!" I hollered, squandering most of my pidgin Vietnamese calling the ARVN a filthy cowardly dog and ordering him to stop.

He kept splishing away from the dawn, toward the dark, blessed anonymity of the exodus.

At first I thought my own murderous panic had spiraled out after the ARVN because his head burst softly like a roman candle.

"Nice shootin', Tex!"

I wheeled around. Efrem had said that to Mark, who grinned and blew across the barrel of his flare pistol like a movie cowboy.

"You asshole!" Bogie paced back and forth. He was distressed, but nothing compared to the other two ARVN.

"Goddamn it!" Toño said.

"You see that?" said Efrem. He was training his weapon on the frightened ARVN as if he thought they might bolt as well. Hoping they would.

"They saw it clear to Hanoi!" Bogie said.

Efrem was delighted. "Slope fuckin' lit up like a fuckin' jackolantern!"

I went over and stood studying the embering head. Couldn't have been more than 14, though now it was hard to be sure, the way the fat was bubbling. I hadn't known. I had never even looked him in the eye. You never looked at the fresh meat. It was easier to lose them that way. But now I could not close my eyes nor look away from the pretty orange glow of the face charring into a skull. *Mark, you twisted sonuvafuckingbitch.*

"Struzick, you're on point!" said Toño as he shouldered past me, squatting to yank the kid's tags. Mark lit a Camel and took up the lead where I had left off.

My finger was itching like mad to go and squeeze a few rounds into my so-called best friend.

In the next instant the sun was dropped on us. The concussion from the homemade mine had us all grabbing real estate.

Ears screaming a highpitched tone, a biting pain in my arm, I touched myself. Blood, but nothing mortal. I bellied forward through the sludge of dawn, through smoke stinging my nostrils. Bogie was pitched face first into the tender rice shoots, a sharp blossom of iron sprouting from his brains right behind his left ear. Mark was down too, on his back, clutching his torn off left leg like we might try to take it away from him.

The day they fitted Mark for his prosthetic leg and shipped him stateside was the last day I saw him for an entire generation.

A lot of folks didn't make it to the twenty five year class

of '71 reunion. But my high school sweetheart Luz Cavazos was there, only by the night of the reunion dance she was Luz Stevens, who had three kids and the hips to prove it. Also a federal judgeship. But as we slowdanced to "Black Magic Woman" I held her close, her sweetbread aroma erasing the years. The more beer I drank, the more it seemed like I had a second chance at all I had lost.

Finally, though, the lights came up in the Sandy Shores Ballroom on the Corpus Christi bay, and I stood blinking in the jittery fluorescence, swaying to the echo of the Doobie Brothers and too many Solo cups of Miller Lite. I saw I was in a room of folding chairs and old people saying goodbye.

"You look like you need a designated driver, Professor."

I turned toward the voice and there he was, hair thinner, a bit of gray, but still Marlboro lean, same old Mark. In his tux you wouldn't even know he had a government issue leg.

"Where's Molly?" I asked.

"Ah, she hates these kind of things. Where's Sandy?"

"No idea. We called it quits three months ago."

"No vale la pena."

"No wayner," I said, and we both smiled.

"But at least this time around," he said, "no custody battle to lose, right?" Sandy and I had scrupulously avoided having kids.

"Thanks, that makes me feel much better."

"Come on, I just meant—"

"Forget it. You should see Laila. Y'know, she's going to be eight in September."

"No shit?"

"She's going to be tall, like me. I've got a picture of her." I couldn't find it. He watched me fumble in my wallet trying to produce some validation for my life. Where was she? Mark stopped my hand's scrabbling.

"Seriously," he said, "let me give you a lift."

"What, like you're Mr. Clean?"

"I've been sober for two years, three months and seventeen days now."

"Well hot damn for you."

"Don't be an asshole," he said. "I still smoke the mota. C'mon, Mac. You staying at your folks'?"

I read somewhere once that deep down we all have a death wish—screw the much vaunted "survival instinct." Being more primal, the desire to return to the big Nada from whence we came always wins out in the end. It's inevitable. I myself have come to believe nobody ever dies until they want to. Of course, all sorts of things can bring about this desire: wife Number Two dumps you, credit cards all maxed out, tenure denied. Or simple, sad weariness at the smug venality of the world. See, that's your spirit longing to return to the Whole Thing. "Giving up the ghost," as they say. The oriental religions believe all of us are God just pretending to be you and me because God gets lonesome being the only One and Only, and so makes up a blockbuster movie called the Universe. God stars in all the roles, a couple of billion, not a few of them heinous villains. Like the Stones used to say back before they had their blood drained and replaced in Switzerland, it's heads, it's tails, you know?

I feel better when I smoke this cigar and think about how I'll be dead some day and none of this will matter anymore. I imagine dying must feel like an incredible pressure relieving headrush, a relief that will make a body cry with joy.

But that night just last June, riding with Mark Struzick toward the house of my father and mother, neither Mark nor I saying what was really on our mind, when that other car topped the low rise along Ennis Joslin Road, and its headlights on high beam made me squint, I recognized the blinding brightness was shining Kali, wearing her necklace of severed heads, and it dawned on me what Mark was about, who he really was, and at that moment of truth I did not cry with joy or relief or embrace Kali's ecstasy which is above all pain and pleasure, above all notions of good and evil; no, man, I clawed like the devil at that buckle fastening my seatbelt.

If Mark hadn't been distracted by me scrambling into the back seat, *maybe* he *might* have noticed the drunk driver crossing the yellow stripe in time to take evasive action.

I think he had the time. But honestly? I can't say for sure. I was in duck and cover mode back down on the floorboard when the light became the roaring thunder of Mark's V-8 engine being rammed right up into the front seat where I had been sitting.

The medics focused most of their immediate efforts on me, since I was losing so much blood. Mark had on his shoulder harness, but the crash had swung his head against the corner pillar of the windshield, crushing his temple. By the time they took care of him, the pressure buildup had destroyed his optic nerves.

When you are young you see only the sturdy oaks, the separate events of your own little life. Not until after you tuck several decades under your belt do you glimpse the forest, do the darkly mottled and gnarled branches reveal the patterns of your existence. In 1972 I wanted to kill that scared Vietnamese kid soldier. Maybe Mark was just taking my sin upon his own flesh. My personal scapegoat. Or was he my bungling devil, who failed in his mission to lead me down the path of perdition? Perhaps I'm *his* devil, or maybe his bungling *angel*. Well. No matter how you cut the deck, the fact is we're linked forever, right? I finally figured that out. That's why I sit here every day watching that guy over there as he learns the ropes of negotiating the world with a cane.

Here he comes, right on schedule. You can pick him out at a distance because of the very slight limp from his prosthetic. His slender cane wavers like a feeler, tap tap tap. Comes right by this corner every afternoon with his instructor, waits patiently, then ventures into the busy intersection during the lull when the light changes. I figure I'm simply

THE EXTINCTION OF RHINOS IN MEXICO

required to keep an eye on him in case he needs help crossing over. No obligation to say a thing. So mum's the word, hey? Sure you don't want a cigar?

ABOUT THE AUTHOR

Stephen Blackburn was a James Michener Fellow in screenwriting and fiction 1995-1997. He grew up in Corpus Christi, Texas, and graduated from the University of Texas at Austin three times. In Kansas City, Missouri, he was a feature writer and movie columnist ("Notes From the Flyover") for *The Pitch*. His article about the near impossibility of living on minimum wage was reprinted nationally by several publications, including *The Utne Reader*. From interviews and collaboration with noted national homeless organizer and activist Ron Casanova, he wrote *Each One Teach One—Up and Out of Poverty: Memoirs of a Street Activist* (Curbstone Press), which *Booklist* hailed as "an eloquent voice for Americans too often ignored or scapegoated." Blackburn lives in Hollywood, California.

###